wicked winemakers

CENTRAL COAST
SECOND LABEL
–BOOK ONE–

BEAU'S
Beloved

USA TODAY BESTELLING AUTHOR

HEATHER SLADE

Table of Contents

1

Sam

"What in the world?" I muttered when, less than five minutes after I fluffed my pillow and climbed into bed, I heard a loud knock at my door. Several knocks, in fact. Actually, more like pounding.

I picked up the fancy cast-iron omelet pan I'd been given as a gift but hadn't used once, except as a weapon. Not that I'd used it for that, either.

"Go away, or I'll call the cops," I shouted.

"Sam, it's me. Open the door. It's bloody cold out here."

"Argh," I growled. I set the pan down, then momentarily reconsidered. If I did hit Beau with it, maybe he'd learn not to show up again in the middle of the night.

I should tell him I was already in bed, but that wouldn't deter him. Maybe if I said I was sick. No, that wouldn't thwart him, either.

Under normal circumstances, I'd consider following through with my threat and actually call the local sheriff. However, Beau's mother had died a few days ago—on Christmas—and, according to him, he needed his best friend. *Me.*

More likely, I was the only friend who would let him in after midnight; therefore, I'd been promoted to "best" status. If only it came with a salary. Then everything I put up with might be worth it.

I looked up at the ceiling. "I didn't mean that," I said in case there was a high power who'd read my thoughts.

"Sam? Open the door!"

I scowled, flipped the deadbolt, and unlocked the rest of the devices I'd felt necessary to install as a woman living alone.

"Hi, Beau," I sighed as much as said when he swept past me.

"Who were you talking to?" He looked around my one-room-plus-kitchen-and-bath apartment, then back at me.

"No one," I snapped. "I was in bed. *Asleep.*"

Most people would apologize for waking me. Not Beau, though. Instead, he asked me if I wanted anything to drink after he'd gone into my kitchen to look for something for himself.

There should be a picture of him in the dictionary next to the word "entitled." Maybe I'd draw one in and show it to him.

"Did you not hear me say I was in bed?" I motioned to where Wanda, my cat, lay snuggled in the blankets like I wished I was.

He pulled one of the two stools sitting near the kitchen counter out and took a seat, then motioned to the other. When I bought them, I'd thought long and hard about purchasing more than one, especially with how expensive they were. At the time, I told myself I might have visitors occasionally, so why not splurge? Now, I regretted it.

Rather than sitting on the bed, which would only make me want to crawl under the covers more than I was already longing to, I sat next to him.

Space was tight, so he shifted my stool until I faced him, then put his long legs on either side of mine.

He held out the glass of wine he'd poured. "You didn't answer when I asked if you wanted some. We can share."

"No, thanks." I covered my mouth when I yawned. Maybe I shouldn't have. Why be polite when he never was? "I'm really tired, Beau."

"Sleep," he said, motioning to the pull-out couch that served as my bed.

"I will as soon as you leave."

"It wouldn't be the first time you've nodded off when I was here."

"Why *are* you here, Beau?"

The playful look that had been on his face since he walked in quickly morphed into one of sadness. "Can't sleep."

I got it. I really did. In the weeks following my mom's death, I hadn't been able to sleep, either.

"We could watch a movie," I offered.

"You wouldn't mind?"

I shook my head and rolled my eyes. "As if it would make a difference if I said I did."

"What shall we watch?" he asked, grabbing the remote for the flat-screen television he'd purchased then mounted on the wall for me. Actually, it was more for him since I almost never watched it unless he was here.

"You pick," I said like I always did.

While he flipped through the channels, I fluffed my pillow, stretched my arms over my head, then got in bed and pulled the sheet and blanket up to my chin. I rolled to my side and wrapped my arms around Wanda as if she were a pillow. A heated one.

It was always cold at this time of year, more so close to the ocean. I lived a mile away from it, not in one of the grand mansions dotting the shoreline. My apartment was smaller than one room in houses like that, but it was mine—as long as I paid the rent every month—and I loved it.

After I was settled, Beau kicked off his shoes, walked over, straightened the blanket on the other side of the bed, propped up two pillows, and sat down.

"Are you asleep already?" he asked, peering over my shoulder since my back was to him.

"Yes."

He sighed. "I'm a wanker for doing this to you, aren't I?" he ventured, overexaggerating his English accent.

"Yes," I repeated.

"If you really want me to leave, I will."

"Good night, Beau."

I got up once in the night to use the bathroom. The TV was still on, and he was in the same position, sitting up, but sound asleep. I covered him with the extra blanket I kept at the end of the bed for occasions like this and went back to sleep. The next time I woke, shortly after dawn, he was gone.

Rather than getting out of bed, I snuggled the cat, my sole companion when I wasn't at work. I'd heard her meowing at the back door of the wine bar where I worked and had gone out to give her some scraps from the kitchen. When she purred and wrapped herself around my leg, I fell in love.

It had been two years, almost to the day, since I brought the kitten home. I was grateful for her company, especially now that my best friend had married and lived in Mexico the majority of the year. I didn't mind being alone, though. It was exponentially better than dealing with roommates like I'd been forced to do for most of my adult life.

Once my boss promoted me to manager and gave me a raise, I decided to finally get a place of my own. Most of my income went to rent, but it was worth it.

When Wanda shifted out of my reach, I closed my eyes, hoping to catch another few hours of sleep since I had the day off. Normally, I was lucky if I got six or seven in.

This time of year was when I banked as much rest as possible. Stave, the wine bar and tasting room where I worked, was closed from Christmas Eve until the middle of January, so I still had fourteen days before I'd have to get back to what was beginning to seem like a daily grind. I hoped after some time away, I wouldn't still feel that way.

"Not again," I growled when I heard another knock at the door. I jumped up to answer it, not bothering to grab my robe in my haste to give Beauregard Barrett—the most inconsiderate human alive—a piece of my mind.

Instead, I came face-to-face with a man in a uniform. "Samantha Marquez?"

"That's me."

"I need you to sign for this."

Once I had, he gave me a large envelope. The minute he placed it in my hands, a feeling of dread swept over me as if whatever was inside was about to change my life—and not for the better.

2

Beau

My mum was dead. No matter how many times I reminded myself, it still didn't seem possible. If only it were a terrible nightmare I couldn't wake myself from.

I lowered my head when a gust of cold wind blew sand across my face, then raised it and looked out at the ocean.

She'd loved this place, being able to take morning walks by the sea when she and my father visited. While I stayed here often, even had a bedroom of my own, the estate belonged to my older brother, Lavery, whom everyone called Press.

He'd named it Seahorse after he purchased the five-hundred-acre piece of property just south of the Central Coast village of Cambria. It was one of a few such parcels still remaining in the State of California. Shortly after the closing, he'd commissioned an archi- tect to design and build the house I stayed in now. The only thing remaining from the previous owners was a barn. That, my brother had renovated, then brought in the horses he'd otherwise kept at my parents' estate in Napa.

There was nothing like being on horseback with the salty air in your face, no one else crowding the beach, and the sound of waves crashing as you rode beside them. The freedom I felt each time I mounted a horse was like nothing I'd experienced anywhere but here.

I checked the time, wishing it was later than eight, so I could ring Sam and invite her to breakfast as an apology for showing up last night. If I called now, though, she'd be angrier than she had been when she let me in an hour after midnight.

Even when I pulled my car out of the garage here at Seahorse and drove the mile to her place, I knew I should turn around and let her rest. Especially since it was one of the two nights she had off each week. I couldn't, though. If I had, I would've gone mad with my inability to sleep.

Instead, the din of the mindless movie I wasn't watching, coupled with her soft snores and her purring cat, lulled me into the deepest sleep I'd had since I learned my mother died. In fact, the only time I'd slept more than a couple of hours was when I was at Sam's place.

One of these days, I knew she'd turn me away. Maybe I'd show up and she'd tell me she already had an overnight guest. Not that she'd had one in the last year; of that, I was certain. It was only after she gave in to my unwillingness to allow her a moment's peace that she confessed it had been longer than that since she last had a boyfriend.

Her saying it was none of my business hadn't deterred me. Whenever she said it, I reminded her I was her best friend; therefore, the only person permitted to ask such questions. Each time, she'd point out I wasn't her best friend; Addy was. "But you're mine," I'd utter in response.

Her other point, namely why I would want to stay in her one-room flat when I could be here at Seahorse or in the guesthouse I lived in at my parents' Napa estate, usually ended in an argument. The worst was the time I'd offered to get her a bigger place. I'd gone so far as to say I'd buy her a house. It took ten days of groveling after that error in judgment just to get Sam to speak to me again.

It was different since my mum died. And yes, I was an arsehole for taking advantage of the fact I knew she'd not turn me away.

I lay in the sand, looking up at the sunless, cloud-filled sky. "I miss you, Mum," I said out loud, my eyes filling with tears like they always did when I thought about her, talked about her, talked to her. She'd been my rock, the voice I heard in my head, the one person—other than my father—I knew would always love me, no matter the shenanigans I pulled.

I reached for my mobile when it vibrated. I'd blocked everyone from calling me, with the exception of my father and Sam, so I knew it had to be my dad since she would never be up this early unless hell froze over. Which, apparently, it had.

"Good morning, sunshine," I answered.

"Ugh. Where are you?"

"Sitting on the sand. Where are you?"

"Ha, ha. Still in bed, but no longer asleep."

"Why aren't you?" I asked.

"Someone knocked on my door at seven this morning."

At first, I thought she was going to say one. "It wasn't me this time."

"Yes, Beau, I'm aware of that."

"So, um, who was it?"

"A courier. That's why I'm calling. I don't know what to make of the package he delivered."

"What is it?"

"Something legal."

"Would you like me to take a look at it?"

I could almost hear her eyes rolling.

"Sorry, obviously. So, I was waiting until a bit later to invite you to breakfast. Shall I pick you up?"

"I could meet you," she offered.

I shuddered every time I thought about Sam driving the clunker she considered adequate transportation. "How much time do you need?"

"I just got out of the shower, so whenever you're ready. Where do you want to meet?"

"I'll be there in fifteen." I ended the call before Sam could argue further, went inside, and took a quick shower myself.

Before I left, I briefly considered whether I should bypass the override on the main residence's alarm I'd set when I arrived, then thought better of it. If Press knew I was here, he might try to talk me into returning to Napa, something I could not bring myself to do. It had shattered me when I was there for my mother's burial. I'd only been able to remain for as long as necessary before telling my father I had to leave. While he understood, Press had not—something I could not care less about.

As far as he was concerned, his house was as vacant as it always was when he wasn't in residence and fully armed against intruders. Technology, and the ability to render it useless, was a wonderful thing.

"Would you like to look at what you've received before or after breakfast?" I asked when Sam opened her door and glared at me.

"Stop hanging up on me. When the call ends, say goodbye. And don't do it just so you can get the last word." She turned her back to me and stalked over to the bar where, I now realized, I'd left my wine glass last night.

I followed. "Apologies," I muttered, picking it up to wash it.

Sam pulled a thick document from an envelope that sat on the counter. Looking up from the glass I was drying, I noticed the first page appeared to be a letter from a law office.

"May I?" I asked, wiping my hands on the same cloth I'd used for the glass—a habit of mine Sam detested.

Rather than apologize again, I lay the towel on the counter when she set the document in front of me.

I skimmed the first page, then detached it and read the opposite side. "This says you've inherited property."

She nodded.

"In New York, of all places. Who is this woman?" I ran my finger down the page to locate the name. "Cena Covert?"

"I have no idea."

My eyes scrunched. "What do you mean?"

"I've never heard of her."

"Do you have family in New York?"

She shook her head. "Nope."

"Are you certain?"

Sam put her hands on her hips. "Yes, I'm certain."

"There must be some connection. This says, 'I bequeath Samantha Marquez, who resides at—'"

"I know my address, Beau. Get to the next part." Sam walked over and picked up her cat. There was a certain way she held the animal when she was worried. I wondered if she even realized. She motioned for me to keep reading.

"Right. It goes on to say, 'The property at 22 Ostrander Road, East Aurora, New York, including all land, residences, outbuildings, and commercial enterprises it entails.'"

In the next paragraph, the document stated the woman Sam said she didn't know had also left her personal effects, a bank account containing over five hundred grand, and an investment portfolio.

"Wait. There's more," I said, reading the second page. "This also says there's a winery and vineyards on the estate."

Sam nodded. "It's got to be a scam, right? Like, I'm being punked right now?"

"Possibly," I muttered, leafing through the rest of the document. "Quite an elaborate ruse, though."

"It can't be real."

I raised both brows. "It appears it is. One other thing. It's left in trust to you."

"What does that mean?"

"Typically, it's done so no one can challenge the will."

"Who would do something like this?"

I walked over to her, grabbed Wanda, and set her on the floor, then pulled Sam into an embrace. "From what I've read, this makes you a relatively wealthy young woman, Samantha."

She wiped her tear-filled eyes on my shirt. "I don't know what to do. I'm struggling with believing this is real."

"What do you suppose would make it seem more so?"

Sam dropped her arms, took a step away, and shrugged. "I don't have any idea."

"Hmm, what day is it?"

"Of the week or the date?" she asked, grabbing a tissue and blowing her nose.

"Um, either."

"Tuesday."

"We'll have breakfast, then ring them," I suggested.

"And say what?"

"We'll ask for a conference." When Sam shook her head, I shook mine too. "I don't understand. What are you saying no to? Breakfast? Please. I'm famished."

"No conference. We'll just tell them I'm not interested."

"I'm too hungry to argue with you. Once I've eaten, I'll convince you to do this. However, at this moment, I simply don't have the energy."

Sam huffed and walked the ten or so paces it took to get from her kitchen to the apartment's door. She pulled it open and waved me through it.

"Am I leaving?"

"I thought you wanted breakfast."

"I do, but only if you're coming with me."

She followed me outside and down the steps to my parked car, muttering something I couldn't understand.

"What was that?" I asked, glancing over my shoulder.

"There isn't enough coffee in the world to get through Beau-in-the-morning."

I wiggled my eyebrows. "I can name at least a dozen women who would strongly disagree with you."

As she so often did, Sam rolled her eyes.

3

Sam

Never in my life had I seen anyone who could consume more food in one sitting than Beau Barrett. Especially when it came to breakfast.

"Are you headed into hibernation?" I said as he shoveled another helping of pancakes into his mouth.

"Sorry, what?"

"Hibernation. Bears have a feeding frenzy in the weeks leading up to it. They eat something like twenty thousand calories a day."

He wiped his mouth and studied me. "What are you going on about?"

"It's called hyperphagia."

I wasn't sure, but his eyes may have rolled back in his head. "*What* is?"

"How much bears—and you, evidently—eat."

"I'm lost."

"Per usual," I mumbled.

When Beau didn't toss a pithy remark back at me, I looked up at him. He, on the other hand, was staring at something over my head.

"What are you looking at?"

"Nothing. Finish your breakfast," he said barely above a whisper.

When I turned to look, he grabbed my hand. "Keep your eyes on me."

"For God's sake, Beau, who is it?"

"Not who. What."

"Then, *what*?" I was practically screeching.

"Bears!"

"You're such a jerk," I muttered, albeit with a smile.

After we finished eating and returned to my apartment, we placed a call to the law office that couriered the documents. Unfortunately, the attorney handling the case wasn't there and wouldn't be all week.

"Are you sure I can't tell them I'm not interested?" I asked.

Beau took a deep breath and let it out slowly. I appreciated he wasn't being flippant about this like he so often was. "If significant wealth wasn't involved, I would suggest that as an option. As it is, your worst-case scenario, as I see it, is selling once the property, etc., is in your name."

"That feels opportunistic."

Again, he took his time responding. "That might be true if you'd sought this out. You didn't. This woman—Cena—left all her worldly belongings to you for a reason. I'd say you owe it to yourself, and her, to figure out why." He sat back and rubbed his stomach.

"Please tell me you're not hungry again."

He laughed and looked at his watch. "I'm good for at least another hour or two. And…don't roll your eyes. Never mind, too late."

He was right; I had done exactly what he told me not to.

Beau reached forward and put his hand on my shoulder. His fingers kneaded the tightness in my muscles. "What else do you want to do today?" he asked.

"Want versus need. Hmm. Need wins. Laundry."

"Good God, can't you have someone do that for you?"

I scowled. "Are you seriously saying you don't do your own laundry?"

"Of course I do my own laundry."

I was sure there was a caveat in there somewhere, as in doing his laundry meant putting it in a bag for whoever actually washed his clothes, then maybe putting them away once they were delivered clean. However, I'd busted his balls about enough in the last twenty-four hours. He'd get a pass on laundry.

"I need to talk to you about something serious," I said instead.

Beau rubbed his hands together and smiled in a way that reminded me of when I first met him.

"No. I'm serious. This is important."

His face fell. "Yes, Miss Samantha. I'm listening."

"Beau, people are looking for you. They're worried about you."

His expression changed. I'd angered him. "The important people know where I am. Otherwise, it's no one's bloody business."

"Who knows where you are?"

"If you insist on making me say it, you and my father."

My eyes opened wide. "What about Press?"

Beau sneered.

"Okay, not Press. Daphne? Remember her? The love of your life? I'm sure everyone you've deemed not important thinks you're with her in Australia."

"I never once said Daphne was the love of my life."

I rolled my eyes.

"I hate it when you do that."

"I'm sorry, but…never mind."

Beau shook his head. "You've gone this far; you may as well spit it out."

"What about Cru and the, you know, other guys?"

"I don't know what you're referring to when you say 'other guys,' and don't you dare roll your eyes again, or I'll put you over my knee. And if I wanted Cru to know where I was, I would've told him. The truth is, it hasn't been long enough for anyone to even care that I'm gone—whatever that means. Where is it everyone thinks I should be?"

"You have a job, Beau."

"You know as well as I do that this is the slowest time of the year in the vineyard. There's literally nothing to do." He sighed, and his shoulders slumped. "I know it may be difficult to believe at times, but I am a grown-up. I stopped checking in once I reached adulthood. I just want everyone to leave me the fuck alone. Present company excluded, of course."

"There are worse things than having family and friends who care about you. Like not having either."

When I turned away, he put his hand on my chin. "Look at me, Samantha." He waited until I returned my gaze to him willingly. "You have many friends who care about you."

"Not *many*."

"Very well, you have friends who care about you. And, I might point out, you may have family who does as well. Or will do." He glanced at the letter from the attorney. "For example, Cena Covert may be a relative. Perhaps you have others you know nothing about."

"One would think if Cena did have other family, she would have left all her worldly possessions to them."

"Well, all right, I'll concede that as logical. Now, apart from the drudgery of laundry, what else do you want to do today?"

"I need to clean the apartment and run some errands. All things you hate."

Beau smiled. "You're just trying to get rid of me now, aren't you? I'm onto you, Ms. Marquez."

It was all I could do to keep my eyes from rolling. It just came naturally when I was around Beau.

"Well done. It wasn't terribly difficult not to roll your eyes, now, was it?"

"I have no idea what you're talking about." I walked over to the window where Wanda lay. Like me, she was probably wishing the sun would shine.

"Sam?"

I scratched her ears, then picked her up for a cuddle. "Yeah?"

"Regardless of how many friends you have, you know I'm always number one, right?" Beau walked over and rubbed Wanda's neck, then messed my hair. "In case you're wondering what that means; no one on the face of this earth cares more about you than I."

"Thank you, Beau."

He cleared his throat more than once.

"Hairball?" I teased.

He stood up straight and stretched. "I think I'll go for a drive. Join me?"

"Only if you're headed to the laundromat."

"*Laundromat?* There isn't a place here to clean your clothes?"

"If you mean in my apartment, as you know, there isn't. In the building, yes. However, there are ten units and two washing machines. Odds are someone is already using them."

When Beau shuddered, I'd had enough. I walked over and pushed him in the direction of the way out.

"What are you doing?"

"You're leaving, and once you're gone, I'm going to do all the things you hire someone to do for you."

He put his hands on his hips when I opened the door and motioned him out. "That's hardly fair of you to say. You're being awfully presumptuous."

"Really? What kind of laundry detergent do you use, Beau? How about your vacuum? What brand is it? And how, exactly, do you clean your toilets?"

When he didn't respond, I gave him a shove.

"I just told you no one on earth cares more about you than me, and you respond by literally kicking me out of your apartment?"

"I'll see you later, Beau."

"You will? What time?"

"Argh. It's a parting phrase. It doesn't mean I'll literally see you later today. It's just *later*."

Before he could engage me in more ridiculous conversation designed to keep him from being bored and me from doing the things I needed to, I shut the door. When he knocked as soon as it was closed, I ignored him.

My phone rang, but I ignored it too. I was just about to put my earbuds in and find some music to motivate me to clean my damn toilet when I saw Beau's car key fob sitting on my kitchen counter.

"Dammit," I muttered, picking it up and stalking over to the door. I yanked it open and handed it to him, averting my eyes so I didn't have to see the smug look on his face.

"I've figured out just the thing to lift your spirits. I'll be back *later*," he said as I shut the door again.

Not feeling like driving into town, I took my bag of dirty clothes and detergent down to the laundry room and found both washers empty. "Yes!" I said, dumping the clothes on the folding table to sort them.

"Hello, Miss Marquez. Are you starting or finishing?"

"Just starting, Mrs. Jenkins," I said, glancing over my shoulder at her.

"I was hoping I could get my wash done before I have to leave for my *Bridge* game. It's okay, though. You go ahead, dear."

I swept the clothes back into the bag and picked up my detergent. "I'm not in a hurry today. You can go first."

"You are a love. Are you sure you don't mind?"

"Not at all," I said. "Good luck at *Bridge*."

Once upstairs, I tossed the bag on the floor and plopped down on the bed. Wanda jumped up and lay beside me. "Maybe I should just take a nap."

The stress of what to do about my "inheritance" prevented me from doing so. It would likely affect my sleep until I was able to speak with the attorney.

I stared up at the ceiling, thinking about Beau and what he'd said about how much he cared about me. I knew he did, in his way. Which, honestly, wasn't *normal*. The man was all or nothing with everything in his life.

Right now, I was his comfort. All of it, apparently. Soon, that would change. He'd get bored with me and maybe even travel to Australia to see Daphne, who he *had* said was the love of his life once, even if he didn't remember it.

Like me, Daphne served a purpose in Beau's life. Whenever another woman expected more from him romantically than he was willing to give, she became the woman he'd parade in front of them until they got the hint that there was no future with him. I wondered why Daphne put up with it. Maybe, like me, she found it impossible to say no to him.

"What do you think the man has up his sleeve now, Wanda?" I muttered to my cat. When Beau said things like, "I've figured out just the thing to lift your spirits," it could literally mean anything from picking up my favorite muffin from the Olallieberry Diner to, God forbid, some extravagant purchase he was sure would thrill me, but instead, made me miserable.

The worst had been several months ago when he showed up, asking me to go for a drive with him.

"Whose house is this?" I'd asked when he pulled up to an oceanfront bungalow on Moonstone Beach Drive.

"First, tell me if you like it," he'd responded.

After several minutes spent trying to get a straight answer out of him, he'd finally confessed his intention to buy it—*for me*. I'd gotten out of his car and walked home so furious I didn't speak to him for several days. It was only after he promised never to do anything like that again that I relented.

God, I hoped he hadn't conveniently forgotten.

4

Beau

"Merry Christmas and Happy New Year!" read the message on the website of the place where Sam was employed. It went on to say that, in order to allow the staff time to enjoy the holidays, they'd be closed until the seventeenth of January. Which meant my plan was a go.

It took two hours to get all the pieces in place, and that had been no easy feat. I hoped that by the time I finished, Sam would be done with the things she had to do. If not, I could wait. However, not too long, given how early it got dark at this time of year.

My last stop was Seahorse, where I grabbed the bag I kept packed in case I needed to leave at a moment's notice. I set the override on Press' alarm system to turn off in fifteen minutes—plenty of time for me to be out of the house, through the gate, and on the road to Sam's place.

"Hello," I said when she opened the door. I peeked into her apartment to gauge whether she might be ready to leave once I presented my plan. Not that I would necessarily notice the difference, but the place did seem tidier than it had been when I left earlier.

"How did it go at the laundry?" I asked when she waved me inside.

Sam cocked her head. "I doubt you really want to know."

"I do, actually."

She laughed. "No, you don't."

"Either way, I've returned with your surprise."

Her eyes scrunched. "Is it an olallieberry muffin?"

"That is one of them, yes," I said, relieved I'd remembered to stop there to pick some up.

She sat down on what was now her sofa rather than her bed. "You know I don't like surprises."

I took the seat beside her. "I believe what I said when I left was I'd come up with something to lift your spirits."

She sighed. "Please, just tell me."

"We're going to New York to visit your property." I can't say what I thought her reaction would be, exactly;

however, it wasn't that she'd burst out laughing, then continue to do so for what felt like several minutes.

"No," she stated emphatically when her giggles finally subsided.

"What else have you got to do for the next two weeks? Besides, this is important, Sam. It's your inheritance."

"I won't dignify your question about my plans with a response. As far as the property is concerned, I haven't spoken with the attorney yet. It might still be a scam."

"About that…"

Her eyes scrunched a second time. "What?"

"It isn't a scam. The will is valid."

"And you know this, how?" she asked, arms crossed in front of her.

"If you recall, we rang the attorney's office from my mobile. Given the urgency, his secretary got in touch with him, and he returned the call."

Sam got up and walked as far as she could within the apartment's confines, then spun around. "That wasn't your phone call to take. You should've told him to call me directly."

I stood and stalked over to her. "Forgive my confusion. From what I recall, you rang me at eight this morning, an ungodly hour for you, and asked me to come over to assist with the package you'd received."

Her eyes remained on mine, but she didn't speak.

"Thus, I assumed you'd want me to handle the call as well. There's nothing untoward happening here, Sam. I'm merely trying to help."

She dropped her arms. "I appreciate that, Beau. However, as you know, I have not, and will not, ever, set foot on an airplane. Thank you for whatever arrangements you've made, but I won't be going to New York."

"I am aware of your intransigence when it comes to air travel and have made other arrangements."

"Beau…" she whined.

"Samantha," I responded with the same tone. "Come on. When's the last time you took a holiday?" I already knew she never had. "This will be fun. We'll drive to this place, err, Aurora, see what kind of digs Cena Covert handed down to you, then return to California before Stave reopens."

She shook her head. "I can't."

I sighed. "Give me one good reason why not."

"Wanda."

I shook my head. "Already taken care of."

"You hired someone to take care of my cat? This is going too far, Beau. Even for you—"

"I did not hire anyone. She's coming with us. I've arranged for everything she'll need."

It was evident she was trying to manufacture another excuse. Finally, she shook her head. "I can't."

"If you wait, you'll have to take off from work. This is the perfect time to do this. And, I'll remind you, there is a significant amount of money involved, Sam. It would be irresponsible to walk away from that alone."

"What if it isn't real?"

"Then, you and I will have enjoyed a cross-country road trip. The time away will do both of us good."

"Where will we stay?"

I steeled myself from smiling. Sam was about to give in. "I figured we could wing it."

"I don't know…"

I put my hands on her shoulders. "There is every reason to do this now rather than wait."

"You're sure Wanda can come?"

I smiled. "Of course. Who would say otherwise?"

"Can we leave tomorrow?"

"Not a good idea."

She folded her arms again. "Why not?"

"Because 'winging' it doesn't mean 'wait until tomorrow.'" Besides, if I agreed, there was a very good chance she'd change her mind.

"Wait. How are we going to take Wanda? Your car barely fits me."

"Come see." I led her to the front door and out to the second-floor landing, where we could see the SUV we'd be driving to New York, the only vehicle in the parking lot.

Her eyes scrunched again. "Whose car is that?"

"I took delivery of it recently." While the statement I'd said was true, if pressed, I wouldn't be above a white lie or two if necessary. "As you can see, it's plenty large enough for you, Wanda, and me."

"It's almost too big. Won't it cost a fortune to drive it all that way?"

"One, it's electric. Actually, a hybrid. Two, I'll worry about the expenses until your inheritance is finalized, at which time you can pay me back." It was one of those white lies I wasn't above telling. I'd never allow Sam to reimburse a single cent. Regardless of the estate's value, my net worth was easily a thousand times greater.

I hit the button on the key fob, and the rear hatch opened. I'd parked in such a way that she could see inside.

"What's all that?"

"I call it Wanda's car condo. While it's technically an SUV, I prefer the alliteration." There was a bed large enough for three Wandas, several toys, a mat with raised edges for things like food and water, and a place for her to do her business if necessary. While the cat would be able to see us and we could see her, there was a mesh divider that kept her contained in her area.

Sam laughed, and it was music to my ears.

"You remind me of my mum," I said, putting my arm around her shoulders. "Your laugh is nearly identical."

"Beau—"

I leaned closer and kissed her temple. "Pack so we can get on the road."

"There's something I need to say first."

I tensed, hoping she wasn't about to say she'd changed her mind. "Go on."

"Thank you for doing this."

I glowed from somewhere inside. While Sam had always been appreciative of the things I did for her, with the exception of the misstep with the house, this time it felt different. More heartfelt. "You're welcome," I murmured.

An hour later, we were on the road. In order to get to New York and return in time for Sam to be at Stave when it reopened, we had to travel at least five hundred miles each day, if not farther. While Las Vegas wasn't quite that distance from Cambria, it was the only place along the way where it made sense to stop. With minimal breaks, we could easily reach the Strip before nine o'clock.

I'd lowered the second-row seat so Sam could check on Wanda, who surprisingly, seemed very content. The only things in the cat's way were our bags, both of which were smaller than the combined feline accouterments I'd secured.

"She rarely rides in the car," said Sam, who looked behind her no less than once every ten minutes. "Usually, she pitches a fit as soon as I put her in the carrier."

After being forewarned by the woman at the pet store about cats' typical response to travel, I'd gone with her suggestion and purchased a collapsible tote to safely transport Wanda to and from the vehicle.

"You're a good cat dad," said Sam, winking.

I smiled and nodded. "Wanda and I came to an agreement quite some time ago. She's accepted that I care about you as much as she does but am better able to provide niceties for you both—given you rarely let her out of the apartment."

Sam laughed, again reminding me of my mum. While most reminders of her resulted in a stab of pain that felt much like a knife, Sam's laughter was different. It wrapped around me like a warm blanket, and I was filled with a sense of peace.

"I'm jealous."

"Of?" I asked, glancing over at her.

"Wanda has never responded to any of the thousands of questions I've asked her."

"Well, then, perhaps we can get her to talk to both of us on this trip."

Sam turned her head away. "Pathetic that, a lot of the time, she's the only one I have to talk to."

I reached over and squeezed her hand. "From what I recall, that was by design after your last roommate was arrested for drug smuggling."

"I'd forgotten all about that since I wasn't there when the sheriff showed up. But, God, it was pretty bad. Thankfully, the rest of us who lived in the house weren't arrested too."

"Vader knows better. Particularly with you."

"Vader. It cracks me up that you all call him that."

I looked at her with wide eyes. "Have you not had the pleasure of speaking to him on the phone? He sounds exactly like the character." I mimicked Vader's breathing.

"This car, err, SUV, is amazing," Sam said after remaining quiet for several minutes. She ran her hands over the seat's leather. "I love the color. It seems like you only see either white or black cars in California. It's a refreshing change."

Knowing she'd like it, I'd chosen the British racing green exterior, referred to as hunter green by the salesman. I caught myself rolling my eyes, much like Sam did so often when he'd said it. The inside was a rich cognac. I would've preferred oyster if not for two things. First, the automobile maker didn't offer it. Second, this car wasn't for me; it was for Sam. I hadn't quite decided when I would inform her, knowing once I did, an argument would ensue.

I had several rationales lined up for the reveal when it did take place. The main reason was her car was front-wheel drive. She'd never be able to drive it in the snow, if the thing even made it out of the State of California.

"What are you thinking about?" she asked.

"The vehicle. Why do you ask?"

"Your facial expressions make it look like you're arguing with yourself."

"Not at all." I chuckled, reminding myself I needed to pay closer attention to how well I schooled my reactions around this woman.

"Would you like to know where I think we should stop for the night?" I asked once we were halfway to my intended destination.

"No. I'm good with winging it. As long as—never mind."

"What were you going to say?"

"As long as it isn't Las Vegas, but there isn't much else on this road otherwise."

I shook my head. "We are definitely not staying in Vegas." At least not any longer.

5

Sam

Beau was lying about something. Maybe more than one thing. It was easy to tell; his right eye twitched. It was barely perceptible, but I'd known him a long time and had learned to look for it when I thought he was fibbing. I wouldn't confront him about it now, though.

What he'd arranged for this trip, especially everything he got for Wanda, was the nicest thing anyone had ever done for me.

"How did you know the wine bar was closed?"

His cheeks pinkened. "Website."

That made sense. With everyone wondering where he was, I doubted he would've called either of the owners, particularly since they were in his circle of friends.

"Do you think your dad has told everyone not to worry?"

"I've no idea."

"But he knows where you are?"

Beau shook his head. "He knows I'm taking the time away I need. He knows he can call whenever he'd like but, otherwise, not to expect to hear from me any more often than was the case, um, before."

I nodded. "How often was that?"

"There was no pattern. Both he and my mum called when they felt the need to. Or missed me."

I reached over and squeezed his hand like he'd done with me. "I'm sorry, Beau."

"Don't be. I cannot envision a trip more ideal than the one we're on."

"You know which trip wasn't?"

He cocked his head. "There are so many trips to choose from."

I smacked his arm. "When you came to get me after my car broke down a half hour outside of Fresno."

"Ah, yes, in the lovely hamlet of La Rosa."

I nodded. "It was scary. Thank God you got there when you did."

"I didn't feel any safer."

I studied him.

"What?" he asked.

"You didn't let on you were afraid. Not even a little."

"That wouldn't have done, now, would it?"

"At times, you're a better man than you let on to be."

He grimaced. "Only at times?"

"You work overtime to hide it."

He was thoughtful before he spoke. "I once over-heard one of the vineyard workers say Press was the good son."

"Ouch," I commented.

"He went on to say it was too bad I wasn't more like him. Even before I overheard that conversation, I'd always done my level best to be as least like Press as I could."

"How old were you?"

He chuckled. "Seventeen, and even I have to admit I was a hellion."

I didn't recall all that much about Beau's reputation back then, but I did remember he'd always been nice to me. "You taught me to drive."

This time he laughed—hard.

"What?" I asked.

"You were dreadful at it. I did many dangerous things as a teenager. None more so than that."

"Teaching me to drive was the *most* dangerous thing you did?"

He nodded. "And that includes motocross racing, skydiving, and bungee jumping."

"I wasn't that bad."

He raised a brow.

"Maybe in the beginning."

He shook his head.

"You're mean."

Beau laughed out loud. "What I am is hungry."

"I can't believe I'm saying this, but I am too."

"Why don't you see if there's a place to eat coming up anytime soon?"

"Hmm."

"What?"

"I have to find my phone. I hope I brought it."

"You aren't certain if you brought your phone? I cannot believe that."

"Why not? It's not like anyone ever calls me. Outside of work, that is." I checked my pockets, then my purse, then it rang, startling me. "It must've fallen under the seat." I unfastened the belt and looked. Sure enough, that's where it was. I picked it up and swiped the screen. "You called me."

He nodded. "To help you locate it; however, that wasn't the only reason."

"Why else?"

"To remind you that someone does call you. Frequently."

"You don't count."

"Wrong again. I count more than anyone else."

I studied my phone, searching for a place to eat. There weren't many. Also apparent was the lack of places to stop for the night besides Vegas. Before and after were just smaller versions of it.

"So, um, before, I said I didn't mind winging it, but where are we stopping for the night?"

Beau glanced over at me. "You're onto me, aren't you?"

"If you mean our options are limited, then yes."

"I'll confess I was planning to stay in Sin City overnight."

I laughed. "Sorry. I shouldn't have said anything."

Beau shook his head. "No, it's good you did."

"We can stay in Las Vegas."

He reached over and took my hand in his. "I want you to be happy, Samantha."

I wiggled out of his grasp and looked out the passenger window. "Why, Beau?"

"Seems obvious."

But it wasn't. I couldn't recall a single time he'd said those words to me. I turned to look at him. "I'm okay, you know. I mean there are a lot worse problems than *maybe* inheriting a house and, um, other stuff. You don't have to worry about me."

"I'm not."

I laughed again. "Now, you sound more like the Beau I know."

He put the hand that had held mine on his heart. "Ouch."

"Come on, stop this."

The grin on his face was replaced with a frown. "Stop what?"

"This isn't how we are. We're more like siblings who fight a lot, but deep down, we care about each other. Don't get all 'I want you to be happy' on me." I waited for him to respond, and when he didn't, I rested my hand on his arm. "Beau?"

"Since my mum…" He shook his head, then donned a smile that looked as fake as I'd ever seen. "Don't worry, I'm sure it will pass. So, Vegas? Any requests?"

"Food."

"Right. We've lost sight of finding somewhere to stop on the way. We might as well wait at this point."

I was starving, but he was right. Vegas food, regardless of where we went, would be better than anything we got along the way—or at least that's what I'd heard. "We need to find a place that will allow Wanda to stay in the room. Oh, and not too expensive. I'm not the heiress you think I'll be yet."

"I don't know why you insist on bringing up money. You know how I feel about it," he snapped.

My eyes opened wide, and I struggled with what to say in response. After a few seconds, Beau laughed.

"Siblings who fight a lot. That's what you said, did you not? Just bringing things back into your comfort zone."

Who cared about each other. I'd said that too. Except, I loved Beau. I could never tell him, though. He'd take it the wrong way and assume I was after him to whisk me away from a life I didn't like and make me his bride, like every other woman on the face of the earth who'd ever met him. I *definitely* didn't love him that way. As I'd said, we were like siblings. Right?

"God, I'd love to know what you're thinking right now."

I shook my head. "No. You don't."

"You can't be serious," I said later when he pulled into one of the swankiest hotels on the Strip.

"Why not?"

"Wanda? My bank account?"

"Welcome back, Mr. Barrett," the valet who opened his door said. The one who opened mine just offered his hand to help me get out.

"Thank you, my good man," Beau responded, shaking his hand. "We've precious cargo in the back, so if you'll be so kind as to let me secure her first, I'd appreciate it."

I stood by the rear of the SUV, waiting for either valet to react to the species of our "precious cargo," but neither did other than to ask if Beau wanted everything delivered to the room. Which he said he did.

Over the years, I'd witnessed the excesses of his life, but none to this extent. "How often do you come here?" I asked once we'd walked past the lobby and directly into the elevator.

He was studying something on his phone but glanced at me. "Rarely." He scowled when I rolled my eyes.

"Yet they know your name?"

"Well, that's more a matter of ownership."

My eyes opened wide. "You own this hotel?"

"Not entirely."

I shook my head. I didn't want to know what that meant. Until I ate, I couldn't think about anything other than how hungry I was. Maybe that's why Beau consumed so much in one sitting. That way, he didn't have to eat again for several hours.

"I'm getting hangry," I grumbled as much to Wanda, who I knelt down to let out of the soft-sided carrier Beau had put her in, as to myself.

"I've taken care of it," he mumbled, still looking at his phone when the elevator came to a stop.

"Is everything okay?"

Beau raised his head. "Yes. Fine. It's just, um, some side work I've been doing."

The door opened, and instead of a hallway in front of us, there was a living room. "What is this?" I asked.

"The penthouse." He pointed to a table that hadn't been visible until we walked farther inside. "There is your food."

"My food?" I gasped.

Shaking his head, he said, "Ours."

"Since you're distracted, I'll eat, then crash. Which bedroom is mine?"

His eyes opened wide. "Bloody hell. They put us in the wrong suite."

"What does that mean?"

Beau pulled his phone out and walked several steps away. "Right. Many thanks." I heard him say before setting the phone down. "Sorry, the Sultan of Brunei booked the rest of the suites some time ago. The concierge said he 'finagled' this one for me." He shook his head again. "Finagled? Such a strange word."

That statement was a perfect example of why I rolled my eyes so often when I was with Beau.

"Do you mind? Truly?" he asked. "We've, err, shared a bed before. Last night, for example."

I said I didn't, but I did mind. This felt different, not that I could explain why. I was saved from saying more by a beeping noise. "What's that?"

"It means someone wants to access the penthouse via the lift. Most likely, the guys are delivering Wanda's stuff along with our bags."

He pressed a button on the underside of a desk.

I shook my head again.

"What?" Beau asked.

"All this…it's, you know, wild," I said, cradling my cat close to me.

"What are you worried about?" he asked.

"Worried?"

Beau stepped closer and scratched behind Wanda's ear, then rubbed her tummy. "I shouldn't tell you, because it will make you self-conscious, but you always hold your cat this way when you are."

Wanda squirmed, and I let her jump out of my arms. "When I am, what?" Beau didn't take a step back, so I did.

"Worried."

"What I am is hungry."

He waved his arm in the direction of the table that was laden with charcuterie, fruit, and bread. "We can order something else if you'd prefer."

"No. This looks, um, good." I hated how tentative my voice sounded as much as how uncomfortable I felt.

When the valet arrived with our bags and all the stuff Beau bought for Wanda, I found a bathroom and washed my hands. As I dried them, I studied myself in the mirror.

It would've been easy to say I was worried about the inheritance. As in, whether it was real or not, and if it was, what that entailed. That alone was certainly enough to make me feel anxious. However, it wasn't the thing that made me want to snuggle my cat. It was Beau.

As silly as I told myself it was, things felt different between us. Maybe because I was in his space instead of the other way around. In my apartment, I was in charge. If he annoyed me, I could tell him to leave. Half the time, he didn't listen, but eventually—if I pushed hard enough—he'd go.

Here, I felt trapped. It wasn't just his hotel room; it was his damned hotel. And his car. And his money paying for everything.

"You don't have to do this," I said to my reflection. "Turn around and go home." There had to be a bus station in Las Vegas, and while I didn't have a lot of money, I certainly had enough to pay for a ticket plus a car service to get me there. But what about Wanda? Were cats allowed on buses? They were allowed on planes, not that I'd be traveling that way—ever.

Beau was waiting in the hallway near the entrance to the bathroom when I came out, looking as though he'd heard the conversation I had with myself.

"I can't do this," I blurted.

He sighed and nodded. "If you are one-hundred-percent certain you cannot, we'll return to Cambria. I won't force you into this. I will, however, urge you to reconsider. As I said before, I believe you owe it to yourself to find out more about the woman who left all her worldly possessions to you." He shook his head. "I fear if you don't, you'll live to regret it."

"I need my own room. At a different hotel."

Beau cocked his head. "What do you mean?"

I walked into the common area of the suite. "I don't feel comfortable staying here with you." I spoke without looking at him, anticipating the hurt I'd see flash in his eyes and the guilt I'd feel causing it.

"I'll go. It's easier than moving you and Wanda." When I turned, he wasn't looking at me, either. He'd picked up his bag and was walking toward the elevator.

"Wait," I said when he pressed the button to call it.

Beau glanced over his shoulder at me. "It's not an issue, Samantha. Wherever we stay for the remainder of the trip, I'll make sure there are two rooms available. Or, if you'd prefer, I can choose two separate lodging facilities."

"Hang on a minute," I said, hurrying over to him when the elevator door opened. I put my hand on his arm. "I'm sorry. I don't want you to leave. I just…"

"Just what?"

As hard as it was for me to admit how I felt, I knew I had to speak fast, or I'd risk him leaving in anger. "I'm uncomfortable when I'm not in control of a situation. Does that make sense?"

Beau smiled and leaned against the doorway of the elevator so it couldn't close. "As I am abundantly aware. Thus, I will do whatever is necessary for you to feel *comfortable*."

"Why?" I whispered.

"Because I care about you, Sam." He shook his head. "I love you."

I knew what he meant. He loved me the same way I loved him—like a sibling. Except he already had one of those and knew how to act around them. I didn't.

"I don't want you to leave."

"If one of us must, I insist it be me."

"Neither of us has to leave. Besides, if you left, Wanda would be furious with me. I'm just…"

"Go on."

"Freaking out. It isn't you, it's me."

This time, Beau rolled his eyes.

"I've never done anything so, err, spontaneous."

After walking back into the main room of the suite and dropping his bag, he rubbed the back of his neck. "I'm the juvenile in this relationship, err, friendship, so I know how ridiculous this sounds, but please, communicate how you're feeling. We'll figure out a solution together."

I stepped closer and put my hands on his folded arms. "You're not as juvenile as you pretend to be."

6

Beau

If anything, I was more so. God, what a bloody idiot I was.

Somewhere in the last four hundred miles, I'd convinced myself that Sam recognized what I'd believed for years. That she and I were a matched set, her yang to my yin—or vice versa; I could never keep them straight. I'd stupidly told myself she was more than my best friend and that we were a man and woman who shared a connection like none other we'd had with anyone else. My jumping to that conclusion was premature, at best. At worst, I felt things for Sam she'd never feel for me.

It wasn't as though I woke up next to her in the last few days and suddenly realized I found her attractive. I always had. If she'd been the slightest bit interested in me, we would've become lovers eons ago.

But she wasn't. So we hadn't.

After spending almost seven hours riding in the car with her, breathing in her scent, hearing her laugh, listening to her talk, joke, be playful, and of course, give me shit, I'd stupidly decided things had changed between us. I'd even wondered if she'd invite me to slide under the covers with her tonight.

As my mum would say, I spent all the time I should be thinking of others' feelings, caught up in my own. Like all else, I'd decided in a short span of time that Sam finally gave in to her attraction to me—one I knew didn't exist.

I'd vowed not to do anything to ruin my friendship with her by treating her the way I treated so many other women. I needed her in my life, and I'd not risk making a move so wrong it would result in her despising me. I could only thank some higher power—perhaps even my mum—for keeping me from not just making a wrong move, but a horrendous one.

As it was, I could soothe Sam's worries like the best friend I was and keep the rest buried deep inside me, like I had for years. The woman was too important to me to do otherwise.

"If that doesn't suit, we can order something else," I said when I saw her pluck an olive from the charcuterie I'd ordered.

"Since it's the second time you've made the offer, I'm going to take a wild guess and say this doesn't appeal to you."

"Yes, well, I could stand something a bit more substantial." I picked up the in-room dining menu I knew by heart and pretended to peruse it. After setting it down, I walked over to the window that looked out over the Strip.

"I'm sorry, Beau. I'm behaving as though I don't appreciate everything you've done, what you've arranged. You're right when you say I called and asked for help. Then when you gave it to me, I argued."

"No apology necessary," I said without looking directly at her. I could see her reflection in the glass from the corner of my eye. Samantha Marquez, even after a seven-hour car ride, without makeup, and her hair tied back, was fucking gorgeous.

Her moods were evident with just one look into her amber-brown eyes. They sparkled when she was happy but turned glassy when she was sad. If I could, I'd remove the band that kept her hair off her neck, so her long, wavy auburn locks cascaded over her shoulders.

In winter, she usually wore a sweater, jeans, and a pair of Chucks, like she was now. The real treat was in the summer when she'd wear shorts, showing off her willowy legs.

"We could go downstairs to the steak house if you'd like," I said, knowing I had to stop thinking about her glorious gams and how I wanted to trail my fingers from right behind her knee up to—

"Beau?"

My cheeks flushed when I raised my head, feeling as though I'd been caught red-handed, so to speak. "Sorry, can you repeat the question?"

"I'm worried Wanda might destroy this place if I leave her here alone."

I looked over at the docile creature languidly licking her front paw. "I find that hard to imagine."

"You'd be surprised. Cats have claws."

I looked around the room, unsure what to suggest. The carrier I'd purchased for her was quite small. I'd hate to put her in it and leave.

"Wait. I know." Sam picked up the cat and carried her into the lavatory. "One bedroom and three bathrooms," I heard her mutter. "I don't think she'll do too much damage in there," she said, closing the door after depositing Wanda inside.

"Shall I give her some toys to play with?"

Sam laughed. "If you ever have a daughter, you are going to spoil her rotten."

"I've never understood that statement. Fruit spoils, yes? Then it turns rotten. What does that have to do with children?"

My dear Samantha rolled her eyes. "How fancy is this place we're having dinner? Do I need to change?" She bit her lip. "Not that I brought much other than jeans."

"You're perfectly fine. We'll sit at the bar if it makes you feel more comfortable."

"Where are we going?" Sam asked as I led her past the gaming area. Before I could respond, a woman I knew approached.

"Beau? Long time no see," the casino host said. She walked up to me, pressing her bosom against my chest. I put my hands on her arms and took a step back. I would've introduced her to Sam, but I couldn't recall her name. Brooke? Crystal?

"Hello," I said instead. "We were just on our way to dinner." When I put my arm around Sam's shoulders, she bristled.

The woman motioned with her head to the craps table. "How about a game before you go?"

I favored rolling the dice over blackjack or poker, and she knew it. I could get caught up in it for hours.

"Perhaps another time," I said, nodding once before leading Sam away.

"She looks crestfallen."

I shrugged a shoulder. "I've been known to lose significant amounts of money."

Sam rolled her eyes—again.

"Where are we now? How far away is the restaurant?" she asked as we walked past several high-end stores.

"Diversification of income. Hotels on the Strip have become entertainment destinations. Concerts, shopping, and other activities not related to gambling bring in huge amounts of cash."

Her eyes were wide as we walked by a well-known jewelry store. "People win, then buy diamonds?"

I laughed and shook my head. "People lose more and buy diamonds anyway. Most of our guests can afford both."

There was a look of disgust on her face. "While others have food insecurity."

"Come again?"

"People who lack consistent access to enough food for everyone living in their household to eat."

Sam had the ability to make me feel guilty about my family's wealth with the utterance of a single sentence. And while my parents, Lavery, and I gave to numerous charities, there were countless more we could support.

"You're right," I said, feeling ashamed, particularly after saying I'd been known to lose big at the craps tables and knowing there were times when Sam had gone without food when her mother's wages were stretched thin.

We were stopped several more times on our way to the restaurant by people who knew me.

"I hope you don't think I'm being rude by not introducing you, but in most cases, I've no idea who these people are."

Sam raised a brow but didn't comment.

"Here we are," I said, motioning to the entrance of the steak house.

"Oh my God, Beau, I can't eat here," she gasped.

"Why ever not?"

She pointed to her feet. "I'm wearing Chucks."

I shook my head. "I told you your attire was fine."

"Do you even own tennis shoes?"

"Of course I do."

She shook her head. "I've never seen you wear them."

"Of course you haven't. We've never played tennis together."

"Argh." Sam stalked off in the direction from which we'd come.

"Hey," I said, hurrying after her. "I thought you wanted to eat."

"You eat. I'll be fine with what you had delivered to the room."

I raced around and blocked her path, stunned when I saw tears in her eyes. "I've done something to upset you, but for the life of me, I have no idea what it is."

When her eyes darted to the people walking past us, I put my hand on her elbow and led her to the side of the corridor.

"Please tell me what I've done."

She folded her arms. "I don't fit here, Beau. Not just here, but anywhere in the kind of life you lead. More, I don't want to fit. This isn't who I am. I'll never be the kind of person you are."

Her words stung. Worse, they felt like a punch to my gut. "Am I truly that horrible?"

"I didn't say you were. I said I'm different. I'm comfortable in my skin, Beau." She pointed at her shoes again. "In my Chucks. I'll never be like the women who seem to know you quite well, even if you say you don't know them at all. And, as I said, I'd never want to be." She pointed to people walking by. "Her, for example."

I looked at the backside of the woman she'd motioned to, the one wearing five-inch stilettos and a black dress tight enough to look sewn onto her body. "Who would want you to be?"

Sam looked up at me. "No one. That isn't the point."

"What is the point?" Admittedly, I was baffled by this conversation.

"Everyone in that restaurant is appropriately attired. I'm not. Saying I'm 'fine' won't change how uncomfortable I feel."

"There are other options, Samantha. We'll simply—"

"Beau?" Unlike some of the others who'd called out my name, the woman standing in front of me was one I recognized. I'd known her almost as long as I'd known Sam.

"*Daphne?* What on earth are you doing here?"

7

"I'm on holiday." Daphne turned to me. "Sam? How lovely to see you."

"Same," I said when we cheek-kissed. I'd met the woman many times, and she'd always been friendly.

"Go ahead, I'll catch up," Daphne said to the two men and one woman who'd stopped a few feet from us. She looked at me. "Forgive me, but would you please excuse us for a moment?"

"No," said Beau, hooking his arm through mine when I turned to leave. "Whatever you have to say to me can be said with Samantha present."

"Very well." Daphne stepped closer to him. "First, I was so sorry to hear of your mum's passing, and I do wish you would've allowed me—" Her voice broke, and her eyes filled with tears.

As uncomfortable as I'd felt a few minutes ago, this was so much worse. "Please, Beau," I whispered, imploring him to allow me to leave.

He shook his head, then turned back to Daphne. "The arrangements didn't allow time for people to fly in."

She wiped her tears. "As I said, I was very sorry to hear of Susannah's passing. She was like a second mum to me."

"Your sentiments are appreciated."

Beau's tone sounded so cold that I couldn't help wondering what had happened between the two of them.

She leaned closer to him. "People are worried about you, wondering where you are. Frantically, I might add." She looked from him to me, then back again.

While my first inclination was to concur, then to defend myself for being with him and not alerting anyone about where he was, this conversation had nothing to do with me.

"You're exaggerating. My father knows where I am. Otherwise, it's no one's concern."

Daphne stood up straighter and squared her shoulders. "Very well," she repeated. "Perhaps we'll speak another time."

"Good to see you, Daph," said Beau, wrapping his arm around my shoulders. If it wouldn't have embarrassed all three of us equally, I would've jerked out of his hold. He had no right to use me—his supposed best friend—to make his ex-girlfriend jealous.

She looked at me and smiled. "As always, it's so nice to see you." When she returned her gaze to Beau, she scowled, said goodbye, and walked away.

"Shall we?" he asked as though the awkwardness of the last few minutes hadn't happened.

"I'm going back to the room. I've lost my appetite."

His eyes scrunched, and he studied me. "I suppose I owe you an explanation."

I shook my head and picked up my pace. The last thing I wanted was for him to *explain*. I felt stupid for feeling jealous of his relationship with Daphne. Whatever was or had been between them was entirely different than what had ever been between us. We were *friends*. Nothing more. So why did the idea of them having a falling out that would eventually lead to them making up upset me to the point I was near tears? I wasn't interested in Beau romantically. I'd never been. So why would I care if he and Daphne got back together?

Like earlier, I considered what I'd do if that happened while we were still in Las Vegas. Which meant tonight. Would she call? Text? Then would Beau sneak out of the room to meet her? What if I woke tomorrow morning—a ridiculous notion since I probably wouldn't sleep—and he hadn't returned?

I'd go home. Whatever it took to get there. Except by plane, of course. Or with Beau. Then I'd call the lawyer handling the inheritance and tell him there had to be a mistake. I didn't know Cena Covert. I'd never even heard the name, and I didn't want anything from her.

Then, when Wanda and I returned to my apartment, my safe haven, I'd let myself cry in a way I couldn't now. As much as I didn't understand my feelings, if I succumbed to my emotions now, my tears would probably send Beau racing as far and as fast away from me as he could get.

"Samantha, stop, dammit!" Beau shouting at me only made me pick up my pace. "Bloody hell," I heard him mutter as he raced around me and stopped. "What is going on?" he demanded.

"Don't use me to make Daphne jealous," I snapped.

His mouth gaped. "I wasn't."

"You put me in the middle."

"I didn't." His head cocked.

"Go find her. I'm going home." I ducked around him and kept walking. Nothing looked familiar, but I hoped whichever way I went, I'd end up in the hotel's lobby.

Beau refused to relent. Instead of grabbing my arm or standing in front of me, he maneuvered me into a hallway, then put his arms on either side of me so I was trapped against the wall. "Explain yourself," he demanded.

My eyes scrunched. "Let me go, Beau."

He shook his head. "I've spent the last twenty minutes feeling as though I've entered an alternate universe where nothing you say makes any bloody sense. Would you *please* tell me what's got you so rattled?"

"I'm not comfortable here. How many times do I have to say it? I want to go home. I don't care about the inheritance. I don't want any part of it. Money may be what your world spins around, but not mine."

Pain flashed in Beau's eyes, and while my voice was raised, he spoke softly. "I'm sorry for anything I'm doing—have done—to make you feel this way." He shook his head. "We never should've stopped in Las Vegas. You were right when you first said anywhere but here. We'll leave now."

"What? No. It's the middle of the night. And you don't have to leave just because I am."

"What would you have me do? Return to the room and crawl into bed? Sleep the night away? As if that's been possible since my mum died—unless I'm with you. And what will you do?"

"Take a bus."

Beau leaned forward, rested his forehead against mine, then kissed where they'd touched. "We're both emotional, tired, and hungry. Let's tackle the latter, rest, then start over tomorrow."

My eyes met his. "But—"

"Please, Sam. I'm begging you to allow me the chance to make this right."

I was tired. Exhausted, actually. And starving.

"How's a burger sound?" he asked when I didn't say anything.

"Really good."

Beau took my hand and led me down a different corridor and outside. He raised his hand, and a cab pulled up. "Mary's," he said to the driver.

The man smiled. "You don't sound like a local."

Beau shrugged. "I know my way around."

We drove in the opposite direction of the bright lights of the main drag and pulled up to a place that looked like a strip club. Beau smiled. "Trust me, okay?"

As if I had a choice.

Once inside, I nearly clapped with joy. Burgers were being prepared on a flame grill in the open kitchen and smelled so good. And, instead of strippers, there was a drag show taking place on the stage. Beau led me over to the bar, where there were two open seats. "How's this?" he shouted over the noise of the music and the crowd.

"Perfect!"

He smiled, pointed to the tap where I only saw one beer, and I nodded. Beau motioned to the bartender, who thankfully, didn't appear to know him.

"What can I get you two?" she asked when there was a break in the show.

"Two beers. Two burgers," Beau told her.

"You got it." The woman looked at me and winked.

"No menu. You get what you get," Beau explained.

"My kind of place." I turned my stool around to face the stage, waiting for the next act to start. Beau handed me a beer, then clinked my glass with his, and I took a long sip.

"Sometimes, there's nothing better than an ice-cold lager."

"I thought you Brits preferred your beer at room temperature."

He laughed and made a face. "I'll remind you I was born in the States, and therefore, I'm not a Brit per se. And it's hardly room temperature, although I'll admit, sometimes it's too warm for my taste." He took another sip.

"Beau—" I said at the same time he said my name.

"Go ahead with what you were going to say."

I felt my cheeks flush. "I'm sorry about earlier."

He shook his head, took my hand, and squeezed it. "It's me who's sorry."

"Can I ask you a question?" I said when he let go.

Beau groaned. "Get on with it."

"What happened with you and Daphne?"

He took another drink of his beer, then set the glass on the bar. "Honestly? Nothing. We aren't what everyone thinks."

"I've seen the two of you together in the past. Clearly, your relationship wasn't platonic."

"Right. However, not the love of my life, either."

"It seemed as though you were angry with her."

He raised and lowered his brow, took a deep breath, and cocked his head. "Her interruption wasn't ideally timed."

"Beau! She lives in Australia. It isn't like she planned it."

"A mere eighteen hours from here," he muttered.

"Come on, 'fess up. There's something else going on."

He picked up his beer and took another swig. "It was rude of her to ask you to step away." He raised a hand when I opened my mouth to argue. "And to be perfectly frank, I'm tired of being scolded for wanting to be on my own."

I'd done that too. "I'm sorry."

"You, I'll accept it from. No one else, however. Other than my father."

"The only two people whose calls you haven't blocked."

He smiled again. "Precisely." Beau rubbed the stubble on his chin. "Did you happen to see the way the bloke she was with glared at me?"

"I didn't."

"I wanted to tell him I was certainly no threat."

"It's odd she was here, though, wasn't it?"

Beau shook his head. "She loves Vegas."

"Does she always stay here? I mean, if she is staying here."

"If you're asking about this hotel, yes. Her father is also an owner, as is mine."

I don't know why that bothered me, but it did. It was another connection the two had. Which *would* bother me if I was interested in him romantically, and I *wasn't*.

"Here you go," said the bartender from behind us. I spun around, suddenly so hungry I couldn't wait another minute. When I took a bite, I groaned. I picked up the napkin and covered my mouth. "This is the best burger I've ever had."

"I told you to trust me."

We were both quiet, focusing our attention on our food. When Beau finished his, he ordered a second. "Fancy another?" he asked.

"I'm full, but thanks." I should probably leave well enough alone, but I had to ask. "You and Daphne have broken up and gotten back together in the past. What's different this time?"

Beau's eyes bored into mine. "Everything."

8

Beau

I loved Daphne. However, I was not in love with her. I doubted I had ever been. It was a conversation I'd had with my mum that made me realize our so-called relationship wasn't healthy for either of us.

"The two of you use each other to avoid forming attachments with other people. One day, you'll wake up and realize you want love in your life. And while I adore Daph and she's like a daughter to me, a long-term relationship wouldn't work between you. If it was meant to be, it would've happened by now. Let each other go, Beau." The conversation had taken place in early November of last year. God knew the last I expected was for my mum to be gone two months later.

She had been my touchstone. If only I could ring her now and get her advice about Sam. Would she say the same thing, that we were friends and if we were meant to be more, it would've happened by now? Worse, would she accuse me of using her like she had with Daph?

"What are you thinking about?" Sam asked, resting her hand on my arm.

I rolled my shoulders. "My mum."

"I know it's hard. I miss mine too. I can't help but wish she was still alive so I could ask if she knew anything about Cena Covert or how the woman knew me."

I chuckled, but not because I found anything amusing about the conversation. "I find myself wondering if I made a single decision—at least a good one—without her input."

"That wasn't the case for my mom and me. Most of the time, I felt more like the parent than the child."

"I recall."

"Were you talking about your mom when you said everything was different?"

I nodded, but it wasn't what I'd meant at all. Sam was the everything I was talking about. I had to sort out my feelings for her. More than anything, I *needed* her. Was it just the loss of my mother, or was there more to it? Again, if only she was still around for me to ask. But then, if she was, Sam and I wouldn't be sitting in a bar, eating burgers, drinking beer, and watching a drag show. Or would we?

Would she still have called and asked for my help when she received the couriered package? I had no reason to think she wouldn't have. As often as she reminded me Addison was her best friend, not me, she wouldn't have turned to her for help with something like this. Would I have responded the way I was now? Maybe, and that was the issue. Was what I was doing for Samantha altruistic or self-serving? There wasn't anyone I could ask, given one I would have was dead and the other was the woman in question.

Sam covered her mouth and yawned at the same time my second burger arrived. I practically inhaled it, not because I was still as hungry as I had been when we arrived at Mary's, but because I knew how tired she was. I wouldn't be at all surprised if she fell asleep on the cab ride back to the hotel. I signaled the barmaid for the check after Sam refused when I asked if she wanted another beer.

As I predicted, Sam was out within minutes of our departure from the bar. She woke on her own when we pulled into the hotel's valet area.

"Sorry," she muttered with hooded eyes.

After paying the cabbie, I got out, walked around the vehicle, and opened her door. "You're knackered," I said, holding my hand out.

She looked up at me. "I'm not used to getting up at the crack of dawn."

"Among other things."

She raised a brow but didn't bother asking what I meant.

Once off the lift, Sam made a beeline for the lavatory where we'd left Wanda. When she joined me in the common area of the suite, she held the cat over her shoulder, but when she spotted the rollaway bed, she cradled her.

While she slept on the drive here, I'd made arrangements for it to be delivered to the suite. However, looking at it now, I wondered if the sofa would've sufficed. Regardless, I'd sleep on one of them and allow Sam to have the bedroom to herself.

"Where I'll sleep," I said, motioning in the direction of her gaze.

"No, you should sleep in there." She pointed. "It's your room. Actually, it's your hotel. We'll be fine out here."

"Not up for discussion, Samantha. Off you go. We should get an early start tomorrow."

"Right. Early." She looked at the bedroom door, then at the rollaway, where I'd taken a seat.

"Your legs will hang off the end of it."

I smiled, thinking of how they did on her bed. "My favorite way to sleep."

"Okay, but wherever we stay tomorrow night, I'll take the rollaway. Or the couch."

While I nodded, she knew as well as I did that would not be happening.

Once the door closed behind her, I went to the lavatory, mulling over whether I should sleep clothed, like I usually did when I stayed at her place, or in my boxer briefs. What I wouldn't do was sleep naked as I usually preferred. I settled in the middle. Shirtless but wearing a pair of sweats. I was about to turn the light off and lie down when I heard the door open.

"Apparently, Wanda wants to sleep with you. I would've ignored her, but I was afraid she'd scratch up the place."

I looked for the cat, but didn't see her.

"Wait. Sorry. She's back in bed." Sam muttered good night for the second time. A few minutes later, I could hear Wanda making a fuss. At this rate, neither Sam nor I would get the sleep we needed. Not that I was sure I would anyway. Would knowing Sam was just in the other room be the same as lying beside her?

I put my hand on the knob at the same time Sam did. "Shall we just leave it ajar?" I asked.

She glanced over her shoulder. "Oh my God. She's on the bed again."

"I believe she's trying to tell us something." I grabbed the blanket supplied with the rollaway and motioned toward the room. "Business as usual, as they say?"

"I feel bad that you always sleep sitting up," she said when I followed her over to the bed.

"Perhaps, just for tonight, I'll lie down."

"It doesn't have to be only tonight. I never said you had to."

Like at her apartment, Sam slept on the right, and I took the left. Also like the times I stayed at her place, I fell asleep as soon as I heard her soft snores, indicating she was.

"No!" Sam cried, covering her head with the pillow when the alarm on my phone went off at six. If we didn't get on the road by half past, we wouldn't get as far as we needed to today. Given we had to return to California by the middle of the month, even driving eight to ten hours per day would take us a total of ten round trip, leaving Sam only four days to meet with the attorney and get an idea of what the inheritance entailed.

I got out of bed, fed Wanda, took a shower, and dressed. When I returned to the bedroom, Sam was sitting on the edge of the bed, looking no more awake than she had a few minutes ago.

"You can sleep as soon as we're on our way," I said, holding out my hand. She took it and stood.

"I'll just shower." Her eyes perused the room. "Where's Wanda?"

"My guess is post-breakfast nap."

"You fed her?"

I nodded. "And packed the majority of her things. Sans travel litter box, carrier, and a few toys, of course."

Sam stretched her arms over her head and patted my chest as she walked past me. "You're a good dad, Beau."

She was teasing. I knew that. What explanation, then, was there for the warmth that flooded me? If I had to name it, I would call it contentment. I'd be the first to acknowledge I made Samantha crazy more often than not, but she, on the other hand, had a way of soothing me like no one else ever had.

"Are you sure it's okay if I sleep?" she asked when we left the hotel and were on the highway.

"Absolutely. We'll take turns."

"You'll actually let me drive your new car?"

It wasn't mine, but for now, I'd let her believe it was. "As often as you'd like."

"What about the Porsche?"

I cocked my head. "Now, you're pushing it." I was teasing. It was difficult for me to deny Sam anything, particularly since she asked for little to nothing.

"This is nice," she said, pulling the blanket I'd retrieved from the rear passenger seat for her.

"It came with the vehicle."

She snuggled into the pillow I'd also gotten for her and was soon fast asleep. I peered in the mirror and saw Wanda was sleeping just as soundly. "You're a good dad, Beau," replayed in my head as the warm feeling settled over me again.

"Where are we?" she asked, stretching her arms over her head like she had earlier.

"Somewhere in Utah. Where exactly, I'm uncertain."

"Is that right?" she asked, looking at the time display. "Did I really sleep five hours?"

I shook my head. "We're in a different time zone, so only four."

"Sheesh," she muttered, then glanced at her cat before turning back toward me. "Do you want me to drive now?"

I shrugged. "You can if you want to. I don't mind continuing, though."

"If I don't drive, I might fall asleep again."

I laughed. "Better that you don't drive, then."

Her cheeks flushed. "You're probably right. It's really beautiful here," she added, looking at the red-clay landscape of the Utah desert.

"Have you ever been?"

Sam rolled her eyes. "I've never been anywhere."

"You've been to Vegas."

"Now, I have."

"That was your first visit?" I asked, stunned.

"When I said I haven't been *anywhere*, I wasn't exaggerating."

"What about Los Angeles?"

She shook her head.

"Santa Barbara?"

Sam scowled at me.

"Wait. You've been to Fresno. That, I'm certain of."

"Again, *nowhere*."

"You and I went to San Simeon." I anticipated and was rewarded with her signature eye-roll.

"That's less than ten miles from where I live."

"I should've taken you to Napa," I said more to myself than to her. There were many places I should've taken Sam. Why hadn't I? I'd known her most of my life. Good God, I could've taken her to London, where my family still maintained a residence. From there, we could've toured the rest of Europe. I felt like a horse's arse for never offering. On the other hand, given Sam's prideful nature, she likely would've turned me down, anyway.

She rested her head against the seat. "I met your mother once."

My eyes scrunched. "I don't recall you doing so."

She smirked. "That's because you weren't there."

"When was this?"

She counted something on her fingers. "Maybe a little over a year ago?"

I chuckled, shook my head, and squeezed the fingers she'd used to count. "What was the occasion?"

"Your parents were visiting Press, and he brought them to Stave for a wine dinner."

"How lovely. I wonder where I was at the time."

"Australia."

I raised a brow. "You recall that, but not the length of time that's passed?"

"Your mom and I had a conversation about it."

Sam turned her head toward the window and folded her hands on her lap.

"Now, I'm intrigued," I commented, but refrained from saying it was primarily due to her body language.

"We weren't the only two discussing it. Eberly Warwick and Isabel Van Orr were there too."

My jaw tightened. The women were daughters of two members of Los Caballeros when my father was. It was a fraternal order of sorts, in existence for hundreds of years. Its membership was generational. Both my brother and I were current members.

When I'd deigned to appear in a related annual bachelor auction fundraiser that supported the local children's hospital, a bidding war had ensued between Eberly and Isabel. Thankfully, Daphne had realized my plight and drove the bids high enough they both finally gave up. Daph and I had left for Australia the following day. "I see," I muttered, remembering I'd intended to join my parents and brother at that particular wine dinner. At the time, I was relieved to have an out, as they say. Now, I wished I'd been there to see my mum and Sam interact.

"She was one of the nicest people I've ever known."

I looked over at her. "She said the same about you."

She wiped her tears and glared at me. "She did not. You didn't even know we met." Oddly, her gaze was focused on my right eye rather than looking into both of them.

"Correction. I didn't *remember* you'd met. Now that you've reminded me, I recall her expressing the sentiment."

Sam huffed, staring again at only my right eye. What in the bloody hell was that about?

"Where are we staying tonight?" she asked, changing the subject.

"I was hoping to make it as far as Glenwood Springs, Colorado. It's another three hours or so."

"Do you own a hotel there too?"

"Samantha, look at me." When she did, I made a point of rolling my eyes.

"That's not an answer."

"I do not."

She tapped her bottom lip. "Does your father?"

"He does not."

"There's a connection, though, isn't there?"

"It's an hour's drive from Aspen, a place where my family often skied."

She pointed a finger at me. "That's where you own a hotel."

I wanted to deny it, but then I'd be lying, which appeared was what she was trying to catch me doing. "Yes."

"I knew it," she muttered. "Are we staying in one of your hotels every night?"

"I believe we've already determined we would not be tonight." I saw her shake her head from the corner of my eye. "What?"

"Where are we staying tomorrow night, Beau?"

I picked up my mobile. "The code is 062598."

She grabbed the phone and was halfway through punching the numbers in when she stopped. "That's my birthday."

"So it is."

"Did you realize?"

"Perhaps," I said with a noncommittal shrug. What I didn't say, never would, in fact, was that Sam's birthday had always been my password. Given my devices had additional security built in, I had no reason to change it. I liked that it always reminded me of her, and also, I'd never once forgotten to wish her a happy one.

"It's not doing anything."

"Right." She handed it to me, and I held it a few inches from my face.

"Why do you have a password if you also have to use facial recognition?"

"An extra layer of security," I responded. However, it was slightly more complicated than that. This particular device had been given to me when I began consulting with a private security and intelligence firm. Rather than using facial recognition, the device made use of my fingerprint in one place and retina in another. If either weren't scanned simultaneously, the mobile wouldn't operate.

"There," I said, handing it back to her. "You can view our itinerary or at least our options. As I told you yesterday, we're winging it."

"Kearney, Nebraska?"

"I can assure you I own no property in that particular city."

"So, why are we stopping there?"

"It's approximately halfway between Glenwood Springs and Chicago."

Sam slowly nodded. "I see."

"Yes. I am part owner of two properties there. It's part of the same group as the Vegas hotel."

"Your life is too complicated for me."

Actually, it wasn't at all. Other than reading through a few annual reports, I paid little attention to my holdings. That was my brother's job.

"Can I drive now? I'm kind of bored."

"Of course." I pulled off the road when I saw a service area, and we switched places. "Does Wanda need to, you know, do anything?"

Sam shook her head. "She's not a dog."

As if that explained it.

"Wow, this car, SUV, whatever, is amazing to drive," she said several miles down the road. "I don't even want to know what something like this cost." She ran her hand over the displays on the dash and fidgeted with the controls of the panoramic sunroof. "Is there music?"

I hit the media button. "Your mobile is already connected, as is your preferred streaming service."

Her eyes opened wide. "You'd be wise not to let me drive this too much."

"Why's that?"

"I won't want to give it back."

I smiled when she winked, hoping she'd feel that way when she discovered the title was in her name.

"Samantha, may I ask you something?"

She looked over at me and smirked. "Are you seriously *asking* if it's okay to *ask* me a question? When, in all the years I've known you, has it mattered?"

"Fair point. Anyway, do I have something on my face?"

"*That's* your question?"

"Not exactly." I turned my head and pointed to my right eye. "Here, perhaps?"

She glanced over at me, then back at the road. "I don't think so. Why are you asking?"

"You appeared to be studying it, err, me. Well, not me, just my eye."

She nodded.

"You're admitting it." I realized I could check in the mirror on the visor myself. I leaned in but didn't see anything amiss.

"It twitches when you're lying," she said, barely loudly enough for me to hear her.

"It does not."

"Tell me a lie, and see for yourself."

"I can't just come up with a lie on the spot," I said, turning my head so she couldn't see the right side of my face.

She raised a brow. "Did it twitch?"

"No."

"How about then?"

It had. Both times.

9

Sam

We arrived in Glenwood Springs after sunset, had dinner at a cute—but casual—steak house, then called it an early night. We slept the same way we did when Beau showed up at my place late at night, since the room only had one bed. Within minutes of taking a shower and my head hitting the pillow, I fell asleep. When I woke in the middle of the night, Wanda was nestled between Beau and me. Like always, he slept on top of the bedclothes, covered by a spare blanket.

I didn't mind. In fact, I kind of liked it. This adventure we were on was so far out of my comfort zone that having Beau beside me, even knowing he was in the room, soothed me enough that falling asleep wasn't the problem it might otherwise be.

We left early the following morning, and like the day before, once on the road, I slept for at least three hours. With Beau's blessing, of course.

We drove through Kearney, Nebraska, deciding to try to get as far as Lincoln, instead. Given it was the capital of the state, we hoped it meant it had more to offer in terms of restaurants and lodging.

Honestly, I wouldn't have cared. There came a point when my hunger reached a level where I was ready to suggest we find a drive-thru fast-food place. Figuring Beau would be disgusted, I refrained.

"You have your choice of burgers or tacos at the next exit. What will it be? Wait. Don't answer that. Burgers it is," he said, looking at something on his phone.

"Is the taco place closed?"

He shook his head.

"Then, why did you nix it?"

"Think about it. Tacos? In Nebraska?"

"I'm not following."

"The state is known for three things. Agriculture, corn, and beef production. Although they could all be considered agriculture. Scratch that." He took a deep breath. "Nebraska is known for three things. Agriculture, Warren Buffett, and the College Baseball World Series."

By the time he finished that diatribe, I'd gone past the exit. "What does any of that have to do with tacos?"

"It is not known for tortilla production."

"How do you know? The second thing you listed in your initial top three was corn."

"And?"

"Corn tortillas? Corn chips?"

He shrugged. "I suppose you make a good point. However, I'm not in the mood for tacos."

My eyes opened wide. "Why didn't you just say that in the first place?"

"I didn't know I felt that strongly about it then."

"But you do now?"

"It's all the talk about corn." He shuddered. "Not a fan."

"How about pizza?" I asked, pointing at the highway sign indicating we could find it at the next exit.

"That's fine since we're not in Chicago."

I shook my head. "I don't even want to ask."

"*Cornmeal* crust." He shuddered again.

"Snow?" I exclaimed when we were about an hour outside of Lincoln.

"I would call this a light dusting, but yes, it could be defined as snowfall."

Temperatures in Cambria could drop as low as freezing, but that was unusual. Typically, at this time of year, lows were in the mid forties. However, it felt colder simply because of the frigid wind coming off the Pacific Ocean. I'd packed sweaters, sweatshirts, and my heaviest jackets, which Beau assured me would be sufficient. If necessary, he'd said we'd shop for warmer outerwear either in Chicago or East Aurora.

When we arrived at our destination, Beau pulled up as close as he could get to the hotel's entrance and instructed me to go straight inside.

"I can help," I countered before exiting the vehicle.

Beau shook his head. "It's *very* cold, Samantha."

I got out, grabbed a few things, and raced inside behind him, wishing I'd put on the gloves and hat Beau had stashed in the glove box for me.

He set Wanda's carrier on the floor, then brushed the snow from my hair. "Stay put. I'll get the rest," he said, walking out before I could argue. Not that I intended to. The snow was falling a lot harder now, making me wonder if we'd be able to leave tomorrow.

I took Wanda from the carrier and held her in my arms. "This is some crazy adventure we're on, girl-friend." She snuggled her head under my chin.

"May I help you, miss?" an older man who'd come out from behind a closed door asked.

"We're checking in."

He nodded and sorted through several pieces of paper, then walked over to where I stood, waiting for Beau.

"This must be Miss Wanda. May I?" he asked. I shifted her so the man could pet her.

"How did you know her name?"

"We always ask when someone says they're bringing their pet along. We also have some treats at the desk if she's allowed."

"That's so kind, and yes, she's allowed."

He rushed back to the counter and pulled out a bag at the same time Beau came inside, carrying our things and Wanda's. "You must be Mr. Barnaby," he said to the man.

"Just Barnaby, and welcome," he responded, handing me the bag of treats. The two men greeted each other like old friends rather than people who'd just met, as was so often the case with Beau.

"I'll have dinner sent up in thirty minutes," he said after we'd finished checking in.

"Dinner?" I said once we were in the elevator.

"Yes. I took the liberty of ordering for both of us."

I didn't mind. He knew what I liked and didn't.

Like in Vegas, Beau had reserved a suite and there was only one bedroom. I didn't care about that, either. It would've been silly to. We shared a bed in the same way I might with a girlfriend. Except—it *wasn't* the same.

I couldn't say I remembered ever being physically attracted to him before. Granted, I was six years old when we met, but even as we both got older and hung out, I always saw him as a friend. I hated how different it felt now. Hated that my pulse raced every time he touched me. Hated that when he'd slept shirtless last night, I wanted to rest my head on his chest and trace his ink with my fingertip. And those boxer briefs? My God—I'd done everything I could not to look; however, my pussy was still drenched. Mostly, though, I hated the longing I felt, wishing he'd touch me—everywhere.

"I'm going to take a shower if you don't mind," I said once I'd gotten my cat settled.

Beau was studying something on his phone like he had been in Vegas. When he looked up at me, his brow was furrowed. "Why would I mind?"

I groaned, grabbed my bag, and went into the bathroom without responding. When I came out, our dinner had arrived.

He stood, walked over to the table where silver domes covered two plates, and pulled out a chair. Once I was seated, he removed the *cloche* from the opposite plate. "My dinner," he announced, uncovering a cheeseburger and fries. "And yours," he said, doing the same to mine but with an added flourish.

I laughed out loud at the two tacos made with corn tortillas, a generous amount of chips made from the same, along with a bowl of corn salsa.

"Both cravings satisfied," he said, taking his seat. "I attempted to add Mexican street corn, but poor Barnaby was at a loss as to what that was."

"No Nebraska street corn?"

Beau laughed. "I'm afraid that's only available in the summer months."

The following day, we drove as far as Chicago, where Beau suggested we stay somewhere other than the hotel he owned. I assured him I didn't care, and he relented. It had been a long day of driving, and we were both exhausted.

When a steak dinner was delivered to our room, I nearly kissed him. Thankfully, before embarrassing both of us, I thought better of it.

"I'd give nearly anything to know what you're thinking," he said as I took a bite of the most perfect filet I'd ever tasted.

When I groaned, devoured another bite, and murmured, "Practically orgasmic," Beau gripped the edge of the table so tightly his knuckles were white. "Everything okay?" I asked.

"Yes. Fine." He took a large gulp of water, finished his dinner, and announced his intention of taking a shower before going to bed.

I dozed off, waiting for him.

We got an early start the following day and arrived in East Aurora before dark. I had the next four days to look into my inheritance and determine whether or not it was a hoax. If it was authentic, I honestly had no idea what I'd do about it.

Either way, we'd have to leave on our return trip to California by then, or I wouldn't be back in time to reopen the wine bar after our annual holiday break.

I was initially concerned that wouldn't be enough time to find out who Cena Covert was or why she'd named me her beneficiary. Now, I saw our schedule as a blessing, and it had nothing to do with her.

I'd begun counting down the days I had left with Beau, knowing once I got home, we'd both go our separate ways like we always did. Then I'd be able to get the ridiculous notion of him kissing me out of my head. I'd have time to remember who Beau was. Namely, a man I could never fall in love with. Allowing myself to would result in unimaginable heartache because Beau didn't believe in love. He'd told me so often enough. Except when it came to Daphne.

While he might be angry with her over something he didn't want to talk about, I'd seen them together many times over the years, and they were perfect for each other.

Something inside me ached at the thought, but there was no sense being jealous of Daphne. Beau and I would be friends—like brother and sister—for the rest of our lives. He'd never love me in the way I was beginning to fear I loved him.

When he pulled up to the front of the place where we'd spend the next three nights, I was thankful it wasn't snowing. In fact, there was very little on the ground. I got out and walked to the back of the vehicle, retrieving Wanda when he opened the hatch.

"You're deep in thought. And worried," he said, motioning to the way I cradled my cat.

"I just want to get this over with so I can go home," I snapped.

Beau raised a brow.

"Sorry. I'm just…"

"Out of your element."

"Way out of it."

He took Wanda out of my arms, put her inside her carrier, and drew me into a hug. "Think of this as a grand adventure, Samantha. One that could give your life new meaning."

I stepped back and out of his embrace. "I'm not looking for new meaning. I like my life the way it is."

He raised a brow. "You're saying working in a bar and living in a studio apartment are your highest aspirations?"

I scowled. "Watch it, Beau."

He closed the little distance I'd put between us. "While I can understand why you'd assume I'm joking, I'm not. This inheritance can change your life *for the better*. I cannot understand why you wouldn't want that."

"What are you suggesting I do, move to New York? I've lived in California my whole life."

He cocked his head. "No, that isn't what I'm suggesting. All I'm saying is you might want to have an open mind."

I shook my head and followed him inside. While Beau spoke with the people at the front desk, I set Wanda's travel carrier on the floor and took a look at the photographs and display cases showing the history of the inn.

It was called the Roycroft, and I learned it wasn't limited to lodging. It had a five-star restaurant housed inside the main building, and additional structures were scattered around what they referred to as a campus. Many housed studios and shops where resident artists worked and sold their creations. There was also a gift shop, a museum, and a library.

According to what I read, Elbert Hubbard, the man who'd originally constructed the mini community, had been a key player in the Arts and Crafts Movement, which included more well-known men like William Morris and the Stickley brothers.

The furniture in the lobby was marked with the distinctive Roycroft logo, and from what I also read, some of the pieces were worth thousands of dollars.

"Fascinating, isn't it?" said Beau, pointing to the front cover of the newspaper mounted in one of the display cases. "The story of how Hubbard and his wife lost their lives on the *RMS Lusitania* is quite romantic."

I turned to him and scrunched my eyes. "Interesting word choice."

He led me over to a second display case, where another newspaper was mounted. The headline read, "Giant Steamer Hits an Iceberg."

The card accompanying it said Elbert Hubbard had given a eulogy for a couple who'd perished when the Titanic went down. "You knew how to do three great things well. You knew how to live, how to love, and how to die."

Hubbard had gone on to praise Ida Straus, the wife of Macy's co-founder Isador Straus, for giving up her place in a lifeboat rather than be separated from her husband. Hubbard also wrote, "I envy you that legacy of love and loyalty left to your children and grandchildren. The calm courage that was yours all your long and useful career was your possession in death."

What Beau read next brought tears to my eyes. "'Neither appeared perturbed in the least,'" wrote a man who'd survived the sinking of the *RMS Lusitania* after it was torpedoed by a German U-boat. The letter on display was written to Hubbard's son about his parents. "Your father and Mrs. Hubbard linked arms—the fashion in which they always walked the deck—and I called to him, asking what they would do. Mrs. Hubbard smiled and said, 'There does not seem to be anything to do.' The expression seemed to produce action on the part of your father, for then he did one of the most dramatic things I ever saw done. He simply turned with Mrs. Hubbard and entered a room on the top deck, the door of which was open, and closed it behind him. It was apparent that his idea was that they should die together and not risk being parted on going into the water."

I wiped away my tears, embarrassed the story had affected me the way it did. When I looked up at Beau, I saw he'd teared up too.

"That kind of love"—he shook his head—"is once in a lifetime, and that's if you're lucky enough to find the person you'd rather die with than live without."

"The true definition of a soulmate," I said, resting my gaze on the photo of Elbert and his wife, Alice, taken right before the departure of the ship on which they took their last breaths.

Beau sighed. "Shall we?" When I nodded, he picked up Wanda's carrier and motioned to the elevator.

"Should we get our bags?" I asked.

He shook his head. "They're being delivered to the room."

Prior to my adventure cross-country with Beau, the few times I'd traveled, and not on any great distance, I'd always carried my own luggage, given the motels I stayed at certainly didn't offer bag-delivery service.

His words from a few minutes ago replayed in my mind. "This inheritance can change your life for the better," he'd said. While it might, I still couldn't envision asking someone to fetch my bags rather than carry them myself.

When the elevator opened on the top floor, Beau pointed to the right, then used an old-fashioned skeleton key to unlock the door. "Quaint," he murmured.

It opened to a spacious sitting area that, like the lobby, was filled with Roycroft furniture. I rested my hand on the arm of a rocking chair.

"All the pieces are made of ash. Quite valuable," he commented.

"How can you tell?"

His cheeks flushed. "I read the description while I was waiting to check in."

I smiled, happy he'd told me the truth rather than pretend he was an expert on Arts and Crafts furniture.

"I was thinking that, once we were settled, we could take a drive by your property, then have dinner somewhere in the village."

"It isn't my property yet," I mumbled, still unwilling to accept this wasn't an elaborate ruse, as Beau had called it.

"Let's go look at it, anyway. Before it gets dark."

10

Beau

There was something about the village of East Aurora that felt familiar and welcoming. When we drove into town, it seemed like we'd traveled back in time or that we were on a movie set.

While I hadn't shared it with Sam, I was able to find aerial photos of Cena Covert's property online, then discovered a website for the winery that showed adjacent structures.

There was a main residence, a guest cottage, a large barn, a carriage house, a winery, and a tasting room. It was impossible to tell if the photos had been taken recently, but if they were, the buildings appeared well-cared for. The other thing I was able to ascertain was that there didn't seem to be a gate blocking people from entering the property.

"Are you sure this is it?" she asked when I pulled into the drive and saw a large sign that read, "The Lilacs."

I checked the address. "This is the place."

I drove slowly, giving Sam time to take in the ever-greens lining the drive.

When we rounded a bend, she gasped. "This *can't* be it."

In front of us, looking identical to the photos I'd seen online, sat the main residence. "It is," I said, cutting the engine and putting my hand on hers when I saw her eyes fill with tears.

"It's so beautiful," she whispered.

I agreed. The wood-plank siding of the farmhouse was painted white, and black shutters framed each of the windows. Along the front and side was a wrap-around porch. A green standing-seam metal roof looked as though it had recently been redone. While there was nothing on the porch besides one bench, I could envision it with multiple sitting areas, hanging and potted plants, and Wanda stretched out, lying in the sun.

"Would you like to walk around?"

"Can we?"

"I don't see why not." I retrieved the notes I'd made from my pocket. "The estate is comprised of six hundred and fifty acres of land. Fifty are utilized for residences, barns, and other outbuildings, including the winery. Four hundred, or one hundred and sixty hectares, are dedicated to the vineyards. The remaining two hundred acres are woods and trails. And, this especially intrigued me, there is a two-acre stream-fed pond with its own private island, waterfalls, and over a mile of stacked-stone walls."

"What are stacked-stone walls?" she asked.

I looked around until I saw an opening in the trees. "There," I pointed. "It's the low wall that surrounds the property."

"A mile?"

I nodded and cleared my throat. "While that is impressive, I was far more taken with the pond and waterfalls."

Sam motioned to the bench on the porch. "I need to sit down."

I put my arm around her shoulders as we walked over to the steps leading to the front door of the house. "We could peek in the windows."

She shook her head. "I can't. It's already too much."

I sat beside her. "Take a deep breath to the count of five, then let it out to the same count. If necessary, repeat."

Whoever chose the location for the house had done a remarkable job. Not only were the vineyards, wooded areas, and pond visible from where we sat, but the view extended for miles, looking out over rolling hills.

I glanced at Sam to comment and saw she had her hands covering her face. Circling her wrist with my fingers, I pulled one of her hands away. "It's simply beautiful, darling." If Sam noticed my slip, using the term of endearment, she didn't let on she had. In fact, I wondered if she'd heard me at all.

"It's too much," she repeated.

"I'll admit it will take some getting used to."

Sam shook her head. "No. I can't do this, Beau."

"As you said previously. However, as I said, perhaps if you let it sink in, you'll—"

Sam got up, then raced down the porch steps and over to the car. "Take me back to the hotel."

While she'd jokingly made demands, I never heard her issue one as she just had. She was always polite to a fault.

I joined her near the passenger door and opened it, deciding not to push further on her accepting the apparent windfall. Perhaps tomorrow she'd be more open to the idea that, by all accounts, she was about to become a relatively wealthy woman.

"I want to go home," she said before we reached the inn.

"Samantha—"

"This is my decision, not yours. Besides, I'm sure there's been a mistake."

"Are you willing to meet with the attorney handling the estate Monday morning?"

Sam looked away from me and out the window without responding.

"If you still feel this way after the meeting, we'll pack the SUV and embark on our return trip."

"Okay," she whispered, brushing away a tear. "How would I even take care of a place like the Lilacs?"

I covered my mouth with my hand when I couldn't stop myself from grinning. By that statement alone, it was evident Sam was already warming up to the possibilities ahead of her. "I'm sure the attorney can shed light on how Mrs. Covert managed."

Once inside the inn's lobby, something in one of the display cases caught my eye. It was a photo of the sign at the entrance to the estate. "Sam, wait," I said. "You must see this."

She walked over and stood next to me, leaning down to look at the photos shown. "Mr. and Mrs. Manley Covert," she read. Then she repeated the man's name. "It sounds familiar, but manly is also a common adjective."

"One used when talking about me, for example." I winked.

"Uh, no. Never that I've heard." She winked, too, then studied the other pictures. "Look at this."

I leaned in close enough for our arms to touch and breathed in Sam's scent. What would she do if I moved her hair from her neck and kissed the soft spot beneath her ear? Fearing she'd belt me, followed by refusing me entry into our room, I refrained.

It—refraining—was becoming increasingly difficult to do. Especially when I fell asleep with her body next to mine. Dreams of wrapping her in my arms, spooning her, nestling my hardness between the cheeks of her perfect arse, plagued me. I feared I'd do just that in my sleep and send her running as far from me as she could.

"Beau?"

"Pardon?"

"Did you read this?"

I studied the postcard she'd pointed to and read it aloud. "I saw you the night of the dance and think if you ever see me again, you will know me." It was to Mr. Manley Covert, posted to the address of the Lilacs.

"It belonged to his family," Sam murmured.

"So it appears."

When she looked at me and smiled, the longing I felt, wanting to kiss her more than take another breath, had me reeling. It was not unlike the night before, when she'd commented that the steak I ordered for her was "practically orgasmic." A cold shower hadn't helped then, and it likely wouldn't now.

"Excuse me," I heard Sam say to the concierge. "Do you know anything about the Coverts?"

The woman approached but shook her head. "I don't. However, I just started working here. You may have better luck asking the morning staff."

Sam thanked her, and we continued studying what was in the cases. Most of the photos were of Cena and Manley together at various stages of their lives.

"This must be their son," she said, pointing to a snapshot of the two with a baby. Sam leaned in to read the caption. "Hmm. According to this, Manley Jr. was born in 1955."

"Is that date significant?"

Sam shrugged. "He was close to my grandmother's age, but I don't think that means anything."

"I would say any clue should be considered as such."

"I guess."

"Shall we check on Wanda, then find somewhere to eat in the village?" I asked when she straightened and looked around the room.

"I wish I had a picture of her. Or of them."

I hadn't thought to check the website for family photos, but there might be some. "Let's go upstairs. You see to Wanda, and I'll look for photographs."

Sam followed me to the lift, but she seemed deep in thought. If only I knew what about. She seemed to vacillate between interest in learning more about Cena, at least, and not wanting any part of the inheritance the woman had left her.

I wondered how I'd react to similar news. Certainly, it wouldn't have any financial impact. The mystery surrounding the connection was what would intrigue me the most.

Seemingly, there was no link between anyone in Sam's family and Cena's. While I knew little about her father, Madeline, Sam's mother, was born in California and, according to what she'd said in the past, her mom was of Spanish or Mexican descent. "Was your grandmother from Mexico?" I asked.

Sam looked up at me. "I don't know."

My eyes scrunched before I thought better of it.

"My mom didn't like to talk about the past. I always figured it was because she felt ashamed about not knowing who my father was."

"Did you ever meet her?"

"If you mean my grandmother, she died the year before I was born."

Once inside the room, Sam opened the door of the lavatory and picked her cat up. She first cradled her, then changed the position when my eyes met hers.

"My mom never left California. She could barely afford the car she used to get to work."

"Here we go," I said, motioning to my laptop. I took screenshots of the photos I found and sent them via messenger to her mobile.

"Where did you find these?" she asked, studying the images.

"Website. There are also shots taken around the estate."

When Sam approached, I moved to the side so she could get a better look. When she zoomed in on one, I peeked over her shoulder. "The winery?" I asked, not knowing why I had. It was obvious.

"I've never heard of the Lilac Lane label, but that isn't a surprise. We don't showcase out-of-state wines at Stave," she commented.

"Nor have I heard of it." I hadn't yet, but at some point this evening, I'd check industry sites to determine the number of cases produced annually, along with the varietals. As far as the Lake Erie AVA—American Viticulture Area, which encompassed East Aurora— the types of wines made were limited, predominately Riesling and Pinot Gris. Some growers also produced Cabernet Sauvignon and Cabernet Franc.

I glanced back at the screen. Sam had zoomed in on a photo of a pasture where several horses grazed.

"It's lovely, yes?"

She looked up at me and nodded. "I hope there aren't still horses there."

"And if there are, that someone is tending them. Which reminds me, I meant to see if there was an obituary for Cena."

"I found one," Sam muttered.

My eyes opened wide, surprised she hadn't mentioned it.

"It didn't say much other than her birth and death dates. Also that her husband and son died before she did."

"When did she pass?" I asked.

Sam's eyes continued to bore into mine, and she took a deep breath. "She died on Christmas."

"Of last year?" I asked. "Well, it would be, wouldn't it? Given the timing of the solicitor's letter."

When Sam nodded, I understood why she hadn't mentioned the obit. Cena Covert had died the same day as my mum.

11

Sam

"If she'd lived one more day, she would've turned one hundred."

"Wow," Beau mumbled. I wasn't sure if it was because of her age or the fact Cena and his mother had died the same day. It was the reason I hadn't told him I found her obituary even though I knew her date of death would come up eventually.

"Are you still up for a walk in the village?" I asked.

The question seemed to jar him out of whatever he was thinking about. "Of course."

I took Wanda into the bathroom, fed her, then shut the door. "I've been thinking about the postcard Cena sent Manley."

"Yeah?"

"It was probably considered forward back then."

While he smiled, it didn't seem sincere. His pain remained evident in his eyes.

"I'm sorry, Beau."

He cocked his head. "For?"

"Reminding you of your mother."

When he turned and cupped my cheek, it startled me, but I didn't react outwardly. "You remind me of her so often." When he leaned closer, I held my breath, wondering if he'd kiss me—hoping, really. Instead, he rested his forehead against mine. "Everything good in her, I see in you," he added.

"Thank you," I whispered, too stunned by his words to think of anything else to say. I couldn't imagine being bestowed a more touching compliment.

Beau dropped his hand and took a step back. "I have few regrets in life. Perhaps others would suggest I should have many more. However, one is that I didn't spend Christmas with my parents this year."

"The wedding." Noah Ridge and his wife, Seraphina, had chosen the day for their ceremony. Given Ridge and Beau, along with Beau's brother, were all best friends, that's where he was, rather than with his family.

He nodded. "Another is that you and my mum didn't have the chance to know each other better. I feel as though I've known you my whole life, yet the two of you didn't meet until recently. Odd, that."

I shrugged. "It wasn't like we could have sleepovers."

This time when he smiled, it felt more genuine. "Not like we do now. And I suppose you're right. It would've been inappropriate to invite a girl over for a play date." His eyebrows wiggled. He picked up the jacket I set on a chair when we came in and held it for me. "Shall we?" he asked after putting his own on.

"I should get my gloves and hat from the car," I said when we left the room and were about to get on the elevator.

"Hold on." He returned to the room, then came out a minute later holding two hats and sets of gloves. "I remembered to retrieve them earlier."

"Such a gentleman," I said, smiling up at him.

He smiled too, but his brow furrowed.

"I hope I didn't just insult you," I teased.

Beau laughed out loud. "Not at all. It's just your smile…"

My eyes scrunched. "What about it?"

Like earlier, he cupped my cheek. "You remind me so much of her."

Would he kiss me now? God, how I wanted him to.

The elevator door opened, ruining the moment, or perhaps saving me from embarrassing myself further.

No doubt, I was gazing at him the way most women did. Beau dropped his hand, and we stepped inside.

While it was chilly, I didn't feel cold once we walked outside and Beau tucked my arm in his. We'd gone a half a block to where several shops and restaurants dotted Main Street when snow began to fall. Softly, though. That, coupled with the lampposts being wrapped with lit garland, made it feel almost surreal. Banners painted with Christmas scenes hung from each post, and sleighs pulled by horses carried people up one side of the street and down the other.

Like the Lilacs, it all felt too perfect—as though I'd stepped into a holiday card. It was the antithesis of my dismal life in California.

My feelings had been hurt when Beau asked if my highest aspirations in life were to work in a bar and live in a studio apartment. Of course, that wasn't the case. However, I had no idea how to change my circumstances.

I'd grown up poor, living in a community where people like my mom and me worked for people like Beau and his family. There was almost no middle ground between the impoverished and the obscenely wealthy.

In the greater metropolitan area surrounding San Luis Obispo, there was, but not in the village of Cambria.

I'd graduated from Fresno State three years ago with a BS in Agricultural Business, but when I applied for jobs, no one even contacted me for an interview. At the time, I'd considered asking my boss at Stave, Alex Butler, if her family or her husband's needed any help at their wineries, but just like if I'd asked Beau, it didn't feel right. Instead, I worked at the wine bar and was eventually made manager.

Thankfully, because we were so poor, my education had been paid for via financial aid, so I didn't have student loans to reimburse after I graduated.

Maybe I should've tried harder to get a better job, but with my mom's death a couple of years ago, it was easier to stay where I was.

Having no other work experience besides helping my mom clean houses when I was younger, how in the world would I manage a place like the Lilacs? We got sidetracked, talking about Cena dying on Christmas day earlier when I commented that I hoped there weren't still horses on the property. That was another thing I'd have no idea what to do about. I'd ridden a horse—once—and was terrified the entire time.

Beau shifted, dropping my arm, then putting his around my shoulders. "It might help if you talk about whatever is on your mind."

"At the moment, it's horses."

He looked over at the ones pulling sleighs. "They're gorgeous creatures, yes?"

"I know nothing about them. Or about taking care of vineyards, running a winery, or living in a house built over a century ago."

"Most don't, and as I said before, I highly doubt Cena managed it all on her own, especially at her advanced age. It's a matter of hiring the right help, which may already be in place. And that, you have experience with."

He was right, although I wasn't successful at it. Once Addy got married and stopped working at Stave, it had been impossible to replace her. I'd hire people, and then after a few shifts, they either called and quit or didn't show up. What if the same happened with the Lilacs? I wouldn't know how to find people to even interview. Especially since I didn't know a single person here.

Beau squeezed my shoulders. "Whatever else you're thinking, I suggest again talking about it. It may help."

"I don't know anyone here," I blurted.

"You know me."

I shook my head. "You know what I mean."

Beau stopped walking and turned to face me. "I'll admit to being somewhat confused. You *do* know me, Samantha."

"You're right," I snapped. "But when you leave, I won't know anyone else."

"I won't leave."

I rolled my eyes. "Even if I eventually decided to live here, to do this? Don't be ridiculous."

"I will *not* leave," he repeated.

"This conversation is pointless. I'm not staying here or, err, coming back here. If this inheritance is real, which I still don't believe it is, I'll have the attorney sell everything." I knew I sounded callous, but what I'd do wasn't the point.

"If you did, I'd buy it."

"No, you wouldn't." I shook my head and laughed, pulling him to keep walking. "Come on, I'm hungry."

Beau seemed disgruntled, but it was silly to talk about something that hadn't happened yet and likely never would.

"What about this place?" I asked, stopping to peruse the menu posted near the sidewalk in front of a house that had been converted into a restaurant. It looked as though it had been built around the same time as the one at the Lilacs.

"It's fine," he responded.

"I'm surprised you'd agree, given there's corn mentioned as an ingredient in every dish, including dessert."

For the first time in several minutes, Beau smiled. "You do amuse me, Samantha Marquez."

The way he looked at me made me weak in the knees. If only what I imagined I saw was real. The more uninterrupted time Beau and I spent together, the more I found myself falling for him. Heartache. That's where I was headed. Worse, if he realized how I felt, it would ruin our friendship. Instead of being with him sometimes, it would become never. There was no way I could risk it. I'd take what I could get.

Two things happened during the course of our one-hour-plus dinner. First, I ate the best gnocchi I'd ever had. It was served with a Gorgonzola cream sauce, radicchio, and walnuts. Second, by the time we finished, Beau knew everyone who worked at the restaurant by name, and they knew him. He was kind enough to introduce me, not that I'd ever be as memorable as he was.

He'd asked all to whom he spoke about the Covert family, but no one knew them. While some had heard of Lilac Lane wine, most were unaware of the estate.

We received multiple "must-do" recommendations, including breakfast at a bakery on Elm Street, catching a movie at the historic Aurora Movie Theatre—located four blocks from the restaurant—and shopping at Berger's Five and Dime store. "It takes up most of the block. My grandmother took my brother and me there when we were kids. Now, he takes his family. I'll admit I still shop there. Best candy selection in the world," our waiter informed us.

Beau's eyes perked up at the mention of sweets. "Is it open now?" he asked.

"Sorry. They close at six, but they're open on Sundays."

"Don't forget Linger," said a waitress when she passed our table.

"What's that?" I asked.

"An art gallery, but honestly, it's so much more than that. It occurred to me the owner might know the family you asked about. Hers has lived here forever," the woman responded. "Wait, they're closed on Sunday and Monday, so you'll have to wait until Tuesday to talk to her."

Since we had to leave Wednesday, I doubted I'd have time to meet the owner, but I didn't tell her that.

A man seated at another table stood and approached ours. "Somebody said you were asking about the Coverts?"

"That's right," Beau responded. "Do you know them?"

The man shook his head. "Not me, but my father might." He pointed to the gentleman seated at another table. "He can be a little forgetful, but I've found he remembers things from the past more than what's happened recently."

"May we talk to him?" Beau asked.

"I don't want to interrupt your dinner, but I've got to get Pops home soon."

"We're finished," I told him.

Beau motioned for me to go ahead while he settled the check.

"My name is Samantha," I told the younger of the two men. When we reached the table, he pulled out a chair for me and, after I sat, introduced me to his father.

"Henry Allen," the man said, reaching over to shake my hand. "This here's my son, Hank."

"Dad, do you remember the Coverts?"

Mr. Allen shook his head, but I saw something in his eyes. Perhaps the name sounded familiar, but he couldn't recall why.

"They owned the Lilacs, out on Ostrander Road."

"Yes," said the older man, nodding. "Beautiful place."

"Cena Covert recently passed away, and I'm doing some research about the family." The fib was something Beau had come up with, suggesting I might not want to share the real details of why I was seeking information.

"Manley was a mean *sonuvabitch*," Mr. Allen spat. "The old man, not the kid. Actually, not him. Her brother."

"Oh!" I exclaimed. "So you do know them?"

He shook his head. "Nope, don't know 'em."

"Sorry," Hank mouthed.

"They went to that church." Mr. Allen nudged his son. "You know where I mean."

"I don't. Do you recall the name of it?"

"It's on Woodard Road. Services are at nine on Sundays."

"Were you a member of the church, Dad?"

We both smiled when he said he hadn't been.

"What did I miss?" Beau asked, joining us.

"Mr. Allen mentioned a church the Coverts went to," I told him.

"You English?" the older man asked Beau.

"I'm actually not, but I did spend a lot of time there when I was growing up," he responded.

Mr. Allen shook his head. "Get my cane, would you?" he said to his son.

"Looks like that's all the entertainment for this evening," said Hank. I stood when he did.

"It was a pleasure to meet you, Mr. Allen."

His eyes scrunched. "He your husband?" he asked, pointing to Beau.

I smiled. "No. We're just friends."

Hank helped his father from the chair. When they passed by, he hit Beau in the shin with his cane. "You're an idiot if you don't marry her," he muttered.

"Agreed," Beau responded, winking at me.

"You should've told him you were already spoken for," I teased once the two men were out of earshot.

Beau cocked his head. "But I'm not."

I rolled my eyes. "I don't believe for one minute that you and Daphne won't eventually get back together."

"Let's go," he snapped more than said. Rather than motioning for me to go first like he usually did, this time he stalked out in front of me. When we reached the door, he grabbed my jacket from the coat rack and held it out for me.

"I was joking," I muttered.

Beau didn't respond until we were outside. "Whatever was once between Daphne and me is no more. We never planned to marry. We will never marry."

"Overreaction much?" I said under my breath.

Beau stalked toward the gate that separated the restaurant's entrance and the sidewalk. He held it open, but as I went to pass, he grabbed my arm, pulling my body flush with his. "Maybe this will convince you," he said, lowering his mouth to mine.

12

Beau

There were countless times I'd thought about kissing Sam. More, I'd fantasized about it. None had ever involved standing on a sidewalk in a village on the East Coast, snow falling softly around us. Admittedly, it was quite romantic, as opposed to my fantasies, which leaned more erotic.

Her lips were no less soft, her taste no less sweet, the way her mouth opened to mine no less breathtaking than I'd imagined. A feral sound emanated from somewhere deep inside me as my desire for this woman, feelings I'd kept buried for years, coursed through every part of my body.

I kissed her fiercely, my mouth capturing hers. I snaked one arm around her waist, then eased it down to the hollow of her back, drawing her closer to my hardness.

Only the sound of someone approaching jarred me out of the lustful haze I'd so willingly dived into. I left my hand where it was but broke the kiss. Sam rested her cheek against my chest.

Once the person passed, I lifted her chin with my fingers so I could gaze into her eyes. Her cheeks were flushed, and she tightened the grip her hands had on my arms.

"We could catch a movie if you'd like," I offered.

Sam smiled but took a step back. "Maybe tomorrow."

When she turned and walked in the direction of the inn, I followed. "Sam?"

She glanced over her shoulder, but it was dark, and I couldn't read her expression. When I caught up and put my arm around her shoulders like I had earlier, she didn't flinch or attempt to move away. She also didn't say anything. Neither did I.

"How about a nightcap?" I asked once we reached the Roycroft, hoping we could ease the tension I felt building between us.

"I'm really tired, but you go ahead," she said, walking toward the lift.

"Sam? Wait."

She turned around. "Yes?"

"We should talk."

When she took a deep breath and slowly let it out, I wished I'd done as she suggested and gone for a drink on my own.

Her eyes softened, and in them, I could swear I saw pity. "If you mean about the kiss, don't worry. I won't make more of it than it was."

More than it was? It was *everything*. Could she truly be so unaffected by it? "I'm…I…um…"

Sam closed the distance between us and put her hand on my arm. "Come on. Wanda is probably going batty stuck in the bathroom."

"Wanda?"

"My cat?"

"I know who Wanda is."

She smiled. "Good. Let's go."

Apparently, we were going to pretend the kiss had never happened. Or at least that it didn't mean anything.

I couldn't, though, not when I wanted it to happen again. Many times over, in fact. If she wasn't willing to talk about it now, perhaps she would once we returned to our suite.

We were about to enter the lift when I received a message on my mobile. "Excellent news. The solicitor, err, attorney has returned early and is willing to meet with us tomorrow instead of waiting until Monday."

Sam's eyes widened. "What time?"

"At our convenience."

"I'd like to visit the church tomorrow."

"Of course. Whatever you want to do."

"I mean I want to go to the service, Beau."

"Right. Yes. Fine." We were going to church? I couldn't remember the last time I'd set foot in one, other than to attend a wedding.

I unlocked the door to the room and motioned for Sam to go ahead of me, then watched as she hurried to the lavatory to let her cat out. Once she had, Wanda raced in my direction, winding herself around my legs. I reached down and gathered her in my arms.

"She loves you," Sam said, taking a seat in the rocking chair.

"At least someone does," I muttered.

Per usual, the woman I wanted to gather in my arms the same way I had her cat, rolled her eyes.

"Shall I make other arrangements for…"

Sam leaned forward. "For what?"

I cleared my throat. "Alternate accommodations?"

"You can't be…"

"Can't be what?" I asked, somewhat relieved I wasn't the only one unable to finish a sentence.

"It was one kiss. You don't have to worry about me making more of it than it was. If it's making you that uncomfortable, you shouldn't have done it."

"I won't apologize."

"I didn't ask you to." When she stood and approached, it was to take Wanda from my arms. "I've had a long day. I'm tired, and I need rest. If you'd prefer, I can sleep there." She motioned with her head to the most uncomfortable-looking sofa I'd ever seen.

"I don't want that."

"I can't remember which of us said it, but on the way to Las Vegas, we agreed you and I are like siblings who fight a lot, but deep down, we care about each other—"

I cut her off. "It was you who said it after I told you I wanted you to be happy."

"Either way, what happened doesn't change anything. Please don't make it weird." I watched her go into the bedroom and flinched when she closed the door. Not because it had slammed, but because it seemed the perfect metaphor for her shutting down the possibility that we could be more than "siblings who fight a lot."

I sat on the poorly designed but very Roycroft-looking sofa, unsure what to do next. "Don't make it weird," she'd said, which I supposed meant don't talk about it. And certainly don't do it again. *It.* The kiss I'd thought about, dreamed about, had been reduced to a pronoun.

I stared at the wall, wishing more than anything I could call my mum and ask her how in the hell to salvage this…this what? Friendship? Relationship? The trip? My God, at least we'd be together another seven days. I couldn't very well hop on a plane and leave Samantha to drive to California alone, and she'd never agree to fly herself.

I shifted my body, lying down and attempting to get comfortable, but knowing I wouldn't be able to sleep.

13

Sam

Once inside the bedroom, I buried my face in Wanda's fur, trying as hard as I could not to cry.

The minute Beau said we should talk, I knew what was coming. He'd tell me the kiss hadn't meant anything and that he'd never consider me more than a friend. So I said it first. Based on his stunned reaction, I was probably the only woman who'd ever let him down easy before he had the chance to do it to her.

That kiss, though. My God, he was good at it. I shouldn't be surprised. He'd had enough practice. Unlike me, who'd dated three men in my life, none of whom stuck around longer than a few months.

But this thing with Beau? I had no idea what to do about it. If things stayed weird between us, what would I do? I was twenty-five hundred miles from home. What choice did I have other than to drive back with him?

I couldn't imagine subjecting Wanda—or myself— to a five-day bus ride. Or longer. I shrugged and set her on the bed. On the other hand, maybe it would be easier than spending the same amount of time in close quarters with a man who didn't have the same feelings for me that I'd developed for him.

Why in the hell had he kissed me? Was it just to prove to himself he was over Daphne? Not that it proved anything other than that he'd regretted it as soon as it ended.

We should talk. The words replayed in my head. Sticking my fingers in my ears did nothing to stop them. As much as I wanted to flop on the bed and cry, Beau might hear me. Worse, he might come in and check on me. Tell me how sorry he was. Maybe if I took a shower instead, I could cry my heart out, and he wouldn't have a clue.

After unpacking the sweats and T-shirt I'd been sleeping in, along with my toiletries, I eased the door open. When I didn't see Beau at first, my stomach clenched, thinking he'd left. When I heard jostling, I realized he was stretched out on the sofa I'd offered to sleep on. Sort of. He looked more uncomfortable than he had on the rollaway bed he'd asked for in Las Vegas.

I set my things on the rocking chair and crept over to him. "Beau?"

He opened his eyes and looked up at me.

"Come to bed."

He nodded, sat up, and walked into the bedroom without saying a word. After retreating into the bathroom to change, I returned to the bed where Beau sat upright, like he did whenever he stayed at my place. Wanda was stretched out beside him, and his hand stroked her fur. I watched them, waiting for him to look at me. When he hadn't after several seconds, I crawled under the covers with my back to him.

"You can watch a movie if you want to," I said.

When Beau didn't respond, I glanced over my shoulder to see if he was asleep. He was not, and he wasn't looking at me, either. Instead, he stared at the wall.

"You don't have to go with me tomorrow. To church, I mean."

"I'll go."

"Okay, well, good night, Beau."

"Good night, Samantha."

When I opened my eyes, light was pouring in through the window and I was alone in bed. The only sound I heard was that of my own breathing. I checked the time on my phone, fearing I'd missed the church service, but I hadn't. It was only seven.

I rolled out of bed and walked through the open door, happy to see Wanda, but disappointed not to see Beau. I breathed a sigh of relief after returning to the bedroom and seeing his bag was still on the floor, near mine. At least he hadn't left. Or left for good. I was about to duck into the bathroom when I heard the door open.

Beau walked in, carrying two paper cups. "Bonjour, mademoiselle, un café?" he asked in his affected jovial tone of voice.

"Thanks," I said, taking the cup he held out for me.

"As far as church attire—"

"Oh! I didn't think about that. I really don't have anything appropriate to wear."

Beau raised a brow.

"Sorry," I muttered. "Go ahead with whatever you were going to say."

"I took the liberty of having something delivered. It should be here any moment."

"When? I mean, thanks. But when?"

"Last evening."

As if he'd commanded it, someone knocked. Beau set his coffee on the floor and opened the door. A man handed him two garment bags along with two smaller bags.

"Much appreciated," he said, setting the smaller ones on the floor near his coffee and handing the delivery person a tip before closing the door.

"These are yours, I believe. However, if it's a suit and wingtips, they're mine."

"A suit?" I raised a brow and smiled, then took the two bags from him. "Thank you for this."

He bowed. "My pleasure. I hope this makes up, at least in part, for my *faux pas* last night."

Faux pas—an embarrassing mistake. That summed it up, didn't it? At least by Beau's estimation. I felt so stupid. On the other hand, he'd kissed me. While I hadn't pushed him away, I also wasn't the instigator. There was no reason for me to feel the way I was, not that telling myself that changed anything. Just like the kiss. That hadn't changed anything, either. At least I prayed we'd find a way to remain friends.

"I hope you'll forgive me."

My eyes met his. "There's nothing to forgive."

"Right. Well, if I could go back in time…"

Everything he'd said in the last couple of minutes was like a knife in my heart. I'd never want to erase the kiss we'd shared. Never. At least I'd experienced Beau feeling desire for me. Whether he regretted the kiss or not, when it was happening, there was no question he wanted me. There was also no question that I wanted him. So what made him do such an about-face? I'd never know because I'd never ask. I innately knew the answer would hurt as much as everything else he'd said.

"I should shower and get ready. Thank you again for this."

He nodded once. "You're welcome."

I went into the bathroom, started the shower, and pulled the garment bag up to see what Beau had chosen for me. I gasped when I saw the camel-colored wool coat and, underneath it, a white sweater and black-knit pant set. It looked cozy but elegant. I hung both on the hook on the back of the door and removed the tissue covering the items in the other bag. On top was a shoe-box, and inside was a pair of black booties. My size, of course. I removed them from the bag and was about to fold it when I realized there was something else inside, besides more tissue.

I reached in and pulled out a very sexy black bra and panty set. When I held them up to get a better look, a piece of paper floated to the floor. I knelt down and picked it up.

The handwriting was Beau's, and his words stunned me. "A dream is but a wish the heart makes," it read. I flipped it over, and on the back, he'd written, "I'll not lie nor will I apologize. But pray tell me, how can I ever love another when you, wearing this, is what I dream of every night?"

I clutched the note in one hand and reached in to turn the shower off with the other. After taking a deep breath, I opened the door.

Beau was standing in the bedroom, wearing only boxer briefs. His eyes were wide when I held my palm out and he saw the note resting on it.

He shrugged and ran his hand through his hair. "It seems I cannot help but make matters worse." When I stalked over to him, he dropped his arms to his sides. "Samantha—"

I put my hand on the back of his neck, pulling him so I could reach his lips. Before we kissed, I whispered, "Do you really dream about me wearing black-lace lingerie?"

Beau slowly shook his head, brushing my lips with his as he did. "Usually, you're naked." He wrapped his arms around my waist, and his hardness pressed against me. "I need you to be sure of this."

"I am, but, Beau, you're sending me mixed signals. Are you certain this is what you want?"

Rather than answer, his mouth plundered mine.

While Beau was nearly naked, I was fully clothed. I stepped back and was about to remove my shirt when he put his hands on mine. "Wait."

"Wait?" I practically shrieked. I couldn't possibly have misunderstood the note he'd included with my bra and panties, nor when he said I was usually naked in his dreams.

"Hear me out."

I took another step back, willing myself, again, not to cry.

"I want nothing more than to finally fulfill all the fantasies I've had about being with you. However, if you remove your clothes now, it is unlikely I will be willing to let you dress again today or perhaps even tomorrow."

That sounded good to me, but I knew what he meant. I wouldn't have time to visit the church, where I hoped to learn more about Cena, or meet with the attorney this afternoon. We had to leave Wednesday. If we didn't, there would be no one to open Stave after the break.

Beau closed the space between us and cupped my cheek. "Make no mistake, my darling, I will make you mine."

I shuddered with the intensity of his words. *His*. But for how long? I shook my head. I couldn't think about that now.

His brow furrowed. "No?"

"No. Wait. I mean, yes. I want you to…you know."

Beau grinned. "Say it."

"Make me yours."

He leaned forward and nuzzled my neck. "Go and shower. Do not come out until you are fully clothed. And by that, I mean wearing my gift under your outfit. It will drive me mad, knowing you are."

"You do remember we're going to church this morning?"

He groaned. "Of course I do. And, while we're there, I expect the deities will reward me generously for my remarkable willpower."

I shook my head. "No deities. Just one God."

"Do you attend church regularly, Samantha?"

"I used to when my mom was alive. It was important to her."

"I can understand why it would have been."

I wanted to ask if his family had a church they regularly attended, but now wasn't the time. As it was, both Beau and I would have to hurry through our showers if we wanted to make it to the church by nine.

While I briefly considered we could save time by showering together, I immediately nixed that idea. That was the last thing it would do.

"Wow," I commented when Beau walked out of the bedroom in his suit after I'd finished my shower, dressed, and was waiting for him.

"Yeah?" he asked, straightening his tie.

I rolled my eyes. "Yes, Beau, you are very handsome and particularly distinguished looking."

"Distinguished? Is that a euphemism for old?"

I decided not to dignify his question with a response since, per usual, he was only fishing for compliments. "Come on, let's go, or we'll be late."

Thankfully, there was only one church we could find on Woodard Road and its service started at nine. We pulled into the parking lot with more than twenty minutes to spare.

"I'd ask if you'd like to walk around, but it seems much colder this morning than it was last night."

I agreed. The temperature had to have dropped twenty degrees at least. I'd never traveled to a place where it got this cold, not even to the mountains in California. "You said your family skied in Colorado?"

"Yes. In Aspen."

"So you're more used to this weather than I am." I held my hands in front of the heater vents to warm them, dreading getting out of the SUV.

"Stay where you are."

Beau cut the engine, got out, and raced around to my door. "Come on, let's hurry." He put his arm around me, and we rushed inside. Once there, we removed our coats and hung them on the racks provided. Then, like the other people who came in after us had, we stomped our feet on the rubber mats to get as much snow off our boots as we could.

We held hands, walking up the four steps to another set of doors where two women stood, handing out programs.

"I'm Violet Hill. We're so happy you've joined us this morning," said the one closest to me.

"Thank you. I'm Samantha Marquez, and this is Beau Barrett."

The older woman's cheeks flushed when she looked at him. I knew the feeling. Beau was ridiculously good-looking, and actually, no one knew that more than he did.

"Have you recently moved here?" the other woman asked.

Beau said yes at the same time I said no. He cleared his throat. "What we mean is we'll likely make this our home soon."

I stopped myself from raising a brow. Later, though, Beau and I would have a talk about being presumptu-ous. On the other hand, I hadn't been paying attention to see if his eye twitched, indicating he was fibbing. Maybe he had, just to be polite.

We walked through yet another set of double doors and into the main sanctuary. The church was small, perhaps only twenty rows deep, but it was beautiful. Beau led me to a pew almost directly in the middle, and we took a seat. I looked beyond him, and what I saw made me gasp. I quickly covered my mouth but pointed in a way no one could see me do it.

Beau turned his head, and while he didn't gasp, I knew he was as shocked as I was.

There were ten sets of stained glass windows on either side, each bearing a name or names. On the two closest to where we sat, Mr. and Mrs. Manley Covert was etched on one. On the other was Mr. Manley Covert Jr.

Mr. Allen's words from last night repeated in my head. While he had corrected himself, the first thing he'd said was that Manley was a mean *sonuvabitch*. "The old man, not the kid," he'd added. Was Manley Jr. the kid he was referring to? Had he passed away at a young age? The only photo we'd seen in the display case at the Roycroft was of him as an infant.

Something about seeing Cena's name affected me in a way I couldn't describe. It was almost as if I felt I belonged here.

I watched as Beau picked up one of the red hymnals from the pew. He opened it and nudged me. The inscription on the inside read, "Given as a gift to St. John's Lutheran Church by Mrs. Cena Covert in honor of her late husband, Manley."

My eyes scrunched when I looked up at him. He leaned forward. "I half expect that, any minute, she'll come and sit beside us," he whispered.

I nodded. I half expected it too.

I'd never attended a service at a Lutheran church before, so I didn't know if all were as traditional as this one, but it was lovely.

When it ended, Beau and I stood but remained in the pew where we'd sat. Several people stopped and greeted us, although I didn't feel right asking about Cena. Apparently, Beau didn't, either.

The last person who stopped to talk to us was Violet Hill, the woman who'd greeted us when we came inside. "We have coffee hour downstairs. We hope you'll join us."

I looked over at Beau.

"We'd be delighted," he said. "By the way, do you happen to know the history behind the names etched on the windows?"

"I do." She pointed to one on the opposite side of the church. "Walter and Marilyn Huber were my parents. They, like the others whose names you see, donated the money to pay for the windows."

"When was that?" he asked.

"Around 1960, I believe."

"Did your parents know the Coverts?" I asked.

She shook her head. "I don't recall ever meeting them, either. Then again, my husband served in the Air Force, and we moved around quite a lot when we were first married."

"We understand Mrs. Covert recently passed. On Christmas Day, in fact," said Beau.

Her eyes opened wide. "That must have been who the funeral was for several days ago." She leaned forward and whispered. "According to Pastor Woodruff, no one was there."

My eyes met Beau's. "No one?"

"Sad. Dying all alone like that. Anyway, I hear a strudel calling my name."

"Interesting, although I suppose not surprising," Beau said after she walked away.

"And, like she said, sad."

"Hello there," we heard a man's voice say from behind us. "I'm Pastor Woodruff. Welcome to St. John's." He'd removed the robe he had on during the service but wore a black shirt with a white collar.

"I'm Beau Barrett, and this is Samantha Marquez." Beau extended his hand, and the two men shook. "We were just talking to Mrs. Hill about Cena Covert," he said, glancing over his shoulder at the window.

The man's eyes, so warm and welcoming only a moment ago, turned sad. And something else. Dark maybe? "Did you know Mrs. Covert?" he asked.

"No, but we were hoping you might have, or perhaps other members of the church," said Beau.

The pastor shook his head. "She was a recluse for many years after her son passed away. Sadly, I only met her one time, and by then, she was quite ill."

"When did her son pass away?" I asked.

He rubbed his chin. "I don't recall exactly, but it has been three or four years now. I'd suggest you take a walk in the cemetery, but with the amount of snow that's fallen, you won't be able to see much. If you call the church office on Tuesday, my secretary will be able to give you that information. Oh, and that of her daughter."

"Daughter?" Beau and I said at the same time.

The man nodded. "She was a teenager when she passed."

My heart clenched. What a sad life Cena had lived.

"Do you know what happened?" Beau asked.

"I believe someone mentioned leukemia. However, again, my secretary would have that information." Like Mrs. Hill, he invited us to come downstairs for coffee. We thanked him as he walked in the same direction she had.

"That she was a recluse adds another clue."

I nodded at Beau. "You're right. Like so much we're learning about Cena, that she lost her daughter at such a young age is heartbreaking."

"Very much so." Beau turned to look at the windows. I wouldn't have been surprised if he was thinking the same thing I was. Cena and Manley's son was honored with one. Why not their daughter?

"Coffee?"

I shook my head. "Do you think we could meet with the lawyer soon?"

"I messaged that we'd be attending the service this morning, and he suggested I ring him when we were leaving."

We walked out the two sets of doors, and while we put on our coats, Beau called him.

"He'd like us to meet him at the Lilacs," he said, pressing the button to end the call.

On our walk to the SUV, I glanced at the windows. While the names were reversed from the outside, I could still see which bore the Covert's names.

"Who are you?" I whispered while I waited for Beau to open my door.

"I have a feeling we'll soon find out," he said after helping me inside.

14

Beau

I felt as though I'd lived nine of Wanda's lives in the last few days. Two or three today alone, and it wasn't yet noon.

When I woke shortly after dawn like I almost always did, I knew I couldn't let things continue the way they were with Sam. I had to tell her how I felt. If she didn't feel the same, well, I'd have to accept it. What I couldn't do was pretend for another moment that I hadn't fallen in love with her. I knew exactly how much I was risking by doing so. Hers was one of the most important friendships in my life. I just couldn't live another day settling for that alone. And her suggestion that we were like siblings nauseated me.

Last night, while stretched out on the most uncomfortable sofa ever made, I'd requested the help of the concierge via the online chat the inn offered, and after I gave her the sizes and types of attire we'd need, she assured me she'd handle it. When I reminded her my purchases would need to be delivered by seven this morning, she repeated it wouldn't be a problem.

After checking my mobile when I woke up and finding a message saying the items I'd requested were in the office near where we checked in, I went downstairs under the guise of fetching coffee for Sam and myself—not that she was awake yet.

Before returning to our room, I wrote the note I'd tucked inside the lace panties. That alone had made me hard enough that walking to the lift would've been embarrassing if I'd encountered other guests.

Fortunately, by the time I was upstairs and about to enter our suite, fear that I was about to do the wrong thing had my excitement waning.

After speaking with me briefly—and awkwardly, I might add—Sam had gone to take a shower. I hadn't expected her to come out of the bathroom as quickly as she did and catch me in nothing but my knickers. When she'd approached, grasped my neck, and brought my lips closer to hers, I could've sworn I heard angels singing.

As difficult as it was to refrain from making love to her then and there, I knew there wouldn't be enough time for me to show her the depth of my feelings. It was important to Sam that we visit the church the man at the restaurant had mentioned last night. We also had a tentative meeting scheduled with the attorney handling Cena's estate.

That's where we were headed now, and Sam's apprehension was palpable. I reached over and took her hand in mine, holding it the entirety of the drive.

When we arrived at the Lilacs, another SUV was parked near the house and lights inside had been turned on. After getting out, I walked around to open Sam's door. Out of the corner of my eye, I noticed horses in the pasture. I hoped Sam had missed that for now, since it was one more thing that caused her worry.

I put my arm around her shoulders as we walked up the porch steps. Just as we reached the top, a man opened the front door.

"Welcome," he said, motioning for us to come inside. "I'm Paul Creola, Mrs. Covert's attorney."

I shook his hand and thanked him for cutting his trip short, then introduced myself and Sam.

"It's a pleasure to meet you," the man said, studying her as if she looked familiar to him. "I lit a fire if you'd like to begin our meeting in the sitting room."

"Thank you," Sam murmured, following him.

The decor of the house was as I'd expected, and while dated, every piece of furniture had been meticulously maintained, as had the wood floors and the rugs covering them.

I watched Sam glance at the artwork and photos that hung on the walls. Framed images were also displayed on a grand piano in the back of the expansive room.

The attorney motioned for Sam to sit, but she walked over to the piano instead. When she got closer, she gasped.

"What is it?" I asked as she lifted one of the frames.

Her face was ashen. "This looks like me," she said, handing over the black-and-white picture of a baby.

The attorney approached. "That's Blanche, Cena and Manley's daughter."

Sam's hands were shaking, and she appeared in shock. "Let's sit," I said, guiding her to the sofa.

"You do favor her," the man said after we'd taken a seat. "There are other photos throughout the house of her as a child and teenager."

"The minister mentioned she died of leukemia," I commented.

The man nodded. "That was before my time, of course, but it coincides with things Mrs. Covert told me."

"She has no other family?" Sam asked.

"She does not," the man responded.

I glanced at Sam, and her eyes met mine. Something about the clipped way he spoke led me to believe he wasn't being entirely forthcoming.

"You're certain?" Sam asked.

He cleared his throat. "Yes. I'm certain." Rather than look at either of us, he appeared to be staring at the piano. His demeanor suddenly shifted, and he pulled papers from a satchel that sat on the floor near where he'd taken a seat. They were the same ones Sam had received via the courier. "Shall we get to it?"

Like in the car, I took Sam's hand in mine, stroking the back of it with the pad of my thumb. She'd stopped shaking but still appeared unsettled.

"Before we do, what is the connection between Cena Covert and me?" Sam blurted.

Mr. Creola sat back in his chair and sighed. "I'm afraid I can't answer that."

She shook her head, and her eyes scrunched. "You mean to say you didn't ask when you prepared her will?"

"It was one of her stipulations."

"How did you get my address?"

"Mrs. Covert provided it."

Sam removed her hand from mine and folded her arms. I had to admit I was proud of the way she'd bounced back from the shock of the photograph.

"What if there's been a mistake?" she asked.

"If you mean by her leaving everything to you, I can assure you, there wasn't."

"How do you know?" she pressed.

The attorney stood and walked out of the room. He returned with an envelope he gave to Sam. "I didn't find this until after she passed away."

She pulled several photos out, the type private investigators took. Each was of her. Two were outside her apartment, and the others were of her coming and going from Stave. She checked the envelope again, but there was nothing else inside.

Clearly, given Sam believed the photo on the piano looked like her, there was a familial connection. However, what it could possibly be was baffling.

"Since everything was left in trust to you, there is no need to involve probate courts."

"What does that mean?" Sam asked.

"Essentially, once the courts certify the trust, everything will belong to you."

I expected Sam to argue, perhaps say she didn't want it. However, when she didn't say a word, the lawyer stood.

"While I can't tell you how you're related to Mrs. Covert, there are other questions I can answer about the estate. I'd like to suggest we meet at my office tomorrow after you've had time to explore the Lilacs."

"What about the horses? Who cares for them?" Sam, who'd obviously noticed them, asked.

"There is a man who oversees the care of the estate with the exception of the grape-growing operation and the winery. That includes managing the livestock."

"Livestock?" I asked, given it indicated there were more than horses.

"Primarily cattle, along with the horses. Additionally, poultry."

"Poultry?" Sam gasped.

"Chickens and turkeys, is my understanding," Mr. Creola responded.

"You mentioned a man oversees them. What is his name?"

"Wheaton. Cord, I believe. According to what I've recently learned, his grandfather and uncle worked for the Coverts most of their lives. His grandfather died years ago, the uncle very recently. Anyway, that's when Cord took over."

"When did his uncle die?" I asked.

The lawyer's expression darkened like it had earlier. "Sadly, not long before Mrs. Covert."

He handed both Sam and me a business card and asked us to ring him in the morning to arrange a time to meet.

I walked him to the door. "What about the vineyards and winery? You said Cord wasn't responsible for those."

"Mrs. Covert contracted for the management of both. Another grower—Schultz is the name—handles the vineyards as well as wine production and distribution. I can give you their contact information at our meeting tomorrow."

After closing the door behind him, I returned to the sitting room and found Sam studying the photos on the piano. She was holding the one she thought resembled her.

"How are you managing?" I asked, coming to stand beside her.

"It feels like a strange dream." She raised the picture. "This looks so much like photos of me around the same age."

"Beautiful," I murmured, taking it and studying the image.

"How, though?"

"If you're speaking of the familial connection, that is a great mystery."

She pointed to the other photos sitting on the coffee table and shuddered. "Someone took those without my knowledge."

I hadn't taken a close look earlier, so I retrieved them. "Can you tell when they were taken?" I laid them out so Sam could view them collectively.

"More than a year ago. Maybe close to two."

"Odd she didn't contact you," I mumbled.

"Everything about this is odd, Beau. More than odd. It's just…*bizarre*."

"By the way, as he was leaving, Mr. Creola said he left several sets of keys in the kitchen. He also said that, by the end of the week, the Lilacs will be yours."

"I'm sure it will take longer than that."

I shook my head. "I don't believe it will."

When she returned to the sofa I followed.

"I need to call Alex."

Raising a brow, I asked, "For?"

Sam turned to me. "I understand if you have to leave, but I can't, Beau. I mean, I just *can't*." She looked around the room, then back at me. "I hope there are keys to a car included in what you said was in the kitchen."

With my arm around her, I pulled her close to me. "I'm not leaving, so put that out of your mind." A sense of utter peace and contentment washed over me when Sam circled my waist and rested her head above my heart. We fit perfectly. Like two pieces of a puzzle, as so many said about how it felt when they found their life's mate. I'd always thought the phrase annoying, until the moment I felt it myself. I kissed her hair. "Tell me you heard me, Samantha."

I felt her nod. "I did."

"And what did I say?"

"You're not leaving."

I doubt she realized what the depth of my words meant. After all she'd been through the last few days, though, I wouldn't tell her that when I said I wasn't leaving, I meant ever.

"What would you like to do now?" I asked.

"We should get back to Wanda."

"We should do."

"And eat."

I would've preferred to do that first, but it wouldn't take long to check on Sam's cat. On the other hand, being in the suite, in close proximity to the bedroom, it would be painful to refrain from suggesting we spend the afternoon in it. Perhaps I'd wait for her in the inn's lobby.

She looked up at me and smiled, once again warming my heart. "Maybe after lunch, we can visit the Five and Dime, then see a movie?"

"Sounds perfect." It didn't sound remotely so, especially the movie part, not that I'd rain on her parade, as they say.

"Or…"

"Or?" My eyes lit up.

"We could get lunch to go, return to our room, and check on Wanda, but forego the Five and Dime and the movie."

I nuzzled her neck, kissing the soft spot beneath her ear. "And do what instead?"

"I could model your gift."

My eyes rolled back in my head, and I groaned, imagining her in nothing but black lace. As far as foregoing anything, I'd be more than happy to skip lunch as well.

15

Sam

All I could think about now was how much I wanted Beau. I *ached* for him.

I'd happily go without eating if it meant he and I would be alone, naked, and making love sooner. Not that I thought he could. In fact, I was surprised he hadn't mentioned being hungry.

Once in the SUV, I wondered if I was wrong about his need for food. The heat pouring off him, his intensity, God, just the way he looked at me had me burning with desire.

"Beau?"

He raised my hand to his lips. "Samantha?"

"How, um, hungry are you?"

We stopped at a red light, and he leaned over. "Starved as a man could possibly be when he's about to bed the woman he's wanted for years."

For years? Those words alone had me wanting to move his hand between my legs so he knew I wanted him as much or more than he did me.

"If I said I wanted to go straight to the inn, you wouldn't mind?" My voice sounded low and husky.

When the light turned green, Beau pressed the gas pedal so hard the tires chirped. At the inn, he pulled up to the front, got out, and tossed the keys to the valet. When another came around to open my door, Beau nudged him out of his way. "I've got this," I heard him growl.

He grabbed me around the waist and slid me down his body as he lowered me from the seat to the ground.

"I've a mind to put you over my shoulder," he whispered in my ear.

I'd be all for it if it didn't mean causing a scene as he stalked through the lobby. As it was, that he held my hand, practically pulling me after him, drew enough attention.

Once we were in the elevator, Beau crowded me against the wall. My pulse raced, and my hardened nipples chafed on the lace of the bra.

He lifted me as if I weighed nothing, holding my bottom with both hands so his hardness rested between my legs. His lips fell against mine, and he coaxed them open with his tongue. "Put your legs around my waist," he said when the door opened.

Beau somehow managed to get the skeleton key in the lock with one hand while not letting go of me with the other. He kicked the door closed with his foot once we were in the room, then carried me past the bathroom and to the bed.

"I will tend to Wanda. When I return, I want you naked, waiting for me right here, Samantha."

I nodded, fearing if I spoke, anything I said would come out as a groan. After shedding my coat and tossing it on the chair, I put my hands on the hem of my sweater to pull it over my head.

I froze when I heard him say, "Sam, wait," from the other room. He stuck his head in the door. "Not naked. Bra and panties remain on." He stalked over to me. "I cannot wait to kiss you again."

My eyes drifted closed, but opened when I heard my cat meow.

"Drat. Wanda. Be right back." Beau released me and nearly ran from the room.

I toed off my boots, finished removing everything but the lingerie, and rested against the pillow with my legs spread—just a little.

When he returned, he'd removed his suit coat and was unbuttoning his shirt. His belt hung loose, and the zipper of his pants was down partway.

"Can I help?"

Beau's eyes met mine. "Given how long I've desired you, I fear if you so much as touch me, I will explode."

I worried he'd tear his shirt in his haste to remove it, but he somehow managed to leave it intact. Next came his trousers, as he called them. When he pushed them down over his hips, his cock jutted out from his body.

He smiled when my mouth formed a perfect "o," then he moved slowly in my direction like a magnificent beast hunting its prey. I'd seen him shirtless but not without briefs. There wasn't an ounce of fat on the man. His muscled shoulders topped his laddered, ink-covered torso. I remembered wanting to trace the large sun that covered his chest with my fingertips. That would come later. Now, my eyes were drawn to his narrow hips and waist and what lay just below it. My breath caught when he wrapped his fingers around himself and stroked.

"Do you know how long I've wanted you?" The icy blue of his eyes was almost entirely eclipsed by his darkened pupils.

My back arched as though his body beckoned mine. "Beau, please," I begged, holding my hand out to him.

"Patience, my darling. I have waited so very long for this. Let me look at you." He knelt between my legs, spreading them wider, then inched his finger between the lace of my panties and my inner thigh. "You are so wet." His gaze traveled my body. "And so fucking beautiful."

He pinched one of my nipples at the same time he thrust a finger inside me, and I nearly came off the bed. "And finally, *mine*."

Another finger joined the first, and he thrust harder. I was on the edge of orgasming when he pulled his fingers away. My eyes met his, and he smiled.

"Sadly, these must go." Beau eased the panties from my body and tossed them on the floor. "Leave it," he said when I stretched to remove the bra. My hand reached for him instead, but he moved too far for me to touch. "Not yet, my beautiful Samantha."

I nearly cried in frustration.

"First, I need to taste you." He lowered his head, and his tongue caressed my folds.

"Beau," I cried out when he flicked the sensitive bundle of nerves with his tongue, then sucked. I reached for him again, weaving my fingers in his hair, then pulled when pleasure so intense spread throughout my body. It was so powerful I felt as though I might shatter. Beau, though, held me together as he slowly kissed his way up to my breasts, lavishing attention on both through the lace of my bra, then dragged the cups down and out of his way. "Take it off," he said before sucking one nipple into his mouth.

Mindless as I was, I had no idea how I managed to do as he said, but suddenly, the bra was gone and Beau was kissing my lips, then nuzzling my neck. I felt his hardness press against me and arched again, wanting him closer, as close as he could be.

He pressed more but still too slowly. When his mouth returned to mine, I nipped his lower lip.

"So needy. So ready for me." With those words, he thrust once, burying himself deep, pulsing within me. He moved, stroking back and forth so slowly I was ready to grab his behind and push myself against him. Instead, Beau lifted my hips, then pounded into me so hard I had to cling to him.

"Now, Samantha." He roared his release as I screamed his name, squeezing him and digging my nails into the flesh of his shoulders while my body shattered for the second time.

I had no idea when he'd put it on, but when I finally released him and he pulled out, I was relieved to see he wore a condom. I hadn't thought about it earlier as I madly writhed against him.

Beau rolled to his side, but every part of his body still touched mine. Our legs were woven together, and his fingers toyed with my nipples. "So sensitive," he murmured when I tried to move his hand away. "Let me touch you, all of you. Let me make you mine."

I looked up at him and cupped his cheek with my palm. "I already am, Beau."

His eyelids slowly closed, then reopened. "Then I pray you're ready to hear this."

My gaze remained steady on his.

"I'm in love with you, Samantha. I feel as though I have been most of my life."

Beau, who'd told me time and again he didn't believe in love had just uttered the words I'd never dreamed I'd hear him say. And he was telling the truth. My eyes filled with tears, and I brought my lips to his. "I'm in love with you too, Beau."

16

Beau

There were no words to convey the depth of my happiness. If one thing could help take away the pain of losing my mum, it was knowing Samantha Marquez, the woman whose smile reminded me of her, loved me. Not just loved me, was in love with me.

I'd hoped she'd feel that way eventually, but that she admitted to it now stunned me. I wasn't the type of man who easily gave in to insecurity, except with her. Thus, as much as I wanted it, I'd feared a romantic relationship between us would not be possible. I couldn't remember a time in my life I'd felt this happy about being wrong.

My ego wanted to confess our first time making love was more hurried than I would've preferred, but why speak negatively when I couldn't imagine anything more perfect than the way Sam and I fit together? I was back to thinking about the puzzle pieces. She and I fit in a way I never had with anyone else.

There had been other women in my life, most notably Daphne, and I loved her. But I was not *in* love with her nor had I ever been.

My insecure ego was also clamoring for me to ask how long she'd felt this way, when she knew, how she knew, but I kept my mouth shut. Did any of it matter when she was lying naked in my arms?

I was ready for round two when I heard Sam's stomach growl, followed by her giggle. "Sorry," she murmured.

"I'll admit there's not been a time in my life I've missed as many meals as I have these few days I've spent with you." I raised her chin and kissed her. "However, there was something else I wanted more than food."

I felt her body tense, then quickly relax.

"Did I say something wrong?"

"No."

I chuckled. "No? That's it?"

She buried her face in my neck, then kissed beneath my ear.

"Samantha, start talking."

"I'd rather you continue to think I'm a self-sufficient, completely secure woman, with zero self-doubt."

"Continue? When did I ever think that?"

She pinched my side.

I wished she'd look at me rather than hide. "Come on, out with it. Shatter my illusions."

"You said you were in love with me."

"That's right. Head over heels, in fact. And you said it back."

"You were telling the truth."

"I was, but I suspect your gaze into my eyes was also to confirm I was."

"Yes and no. I mean, I wasn't looking for it."

"The dratted eye twitch. I suppose the lack of it is as telling as when it happens. However, I fear you're still trying to convince yourself that what I feel for you is real."

"More, that it will last."

"Samantha, please look at me." It took a few seconds, but when she finally did, I breathed in deeply. "Shall I tell you all the reasons I love you? Should I confess how long I've wanted this? Like you, do I dare allow you to think I'm not the self-sufficient, completely secure man you believe me to be?"

"Self-sufficient?" she said, smiling.

"Yes, I suppose that part was a stretch. Either way, I was experiencing the same worry you shared with me. Per usual, you are braver than I and admitted it long before I could muster the courage to do so."

"Beau?"

"Yes, my love?"

"I'm starving."

I laughed and kissed her hair. "Room service or venture out?"

"Room service, definitely."

We made love again while we waited for our food to be delivered, then again after we ate, and again after that.

I had no idea how I'd gone twenty-seven years—or at least fifteen, since I hit puberty—without knowing the exquisite pleasure of being with Sam. It was akin to making love for the very first time.

I wouldn't say she was the most experienced lover I'd ever been with, but that didn't change how absolutely, magnificently perfect being inside her felt. Watching her face when she orgasmed was breathtaking, and in the aftermath, holding her filled me with joy and a sense of peace, knowing I belonged in her arms and she in mine.

"I hate to say this…" she began.

"I have a feeling I'm going to hate hearing it more."

"As much as I want to stay in this room and never leave, I feel as though we should return to the Lilacs before it gets dark. I'm hoping we can connect with the man the attorney said was taking care of the horses."

"I agree with every part of what you've just said, including wishing we could stay in this *bed* and never leave. I mention this specifically, given I don't believe there's a single other piece of furniture in the suite conducive to lovemaking."

"So you wouldn't mind if we went to the Lilacs?"

"Not at all." When Sam shifted her body so it was no longer resting on mine, I immediately wanted her to come back. I rolled out of bed, caught up with her on the way to take a shower, and put my hand on her shoulder. "I fear you'll quickly tire of me touching you."

"Never, Beau."

"In that case, you won't mind sharing a shower."

"If I fit." She winked.

I agreed the enclosure was not overly large, considering I was six feet two and weighed over two hundred and twenty pounds. "I can wait until you're finished."

Sam shook her head.

"You're certain?"

She opened the glass door and pulled me in with her. In order to fit, her body had to be flush with mine, not that I minded.

"Maybe we should rethink leaving," she said, reaching around to grip my arse with both hands.

I rested my forehead against hers, willing my body to settle down. "Do you have any idea how much I love you? Love this?"

"I think I do."

After washing her hair and body, Sam pivoted both of us so she was no longer under the flow of water, then opened the door to step out. I immediately felt a chill that had nothing to do with cold air. I never, ever wanted to be away from this woman. Not for a week, a day, or even an hour. Minutes would be difficult enough.

"Will you tell me if I'm overdoing it?" I asked when I turned off the shower and she handed me a towel.

Her head cocked. "In what way?"

"Too much togetherness."

"Beau, I haven't counted the hours since we went from friends to lovers, but it might be too soon to evaluate how it's working out."

As right as she was, it didn't change the dread in my stomach whenever I considered how I'd feel when the time came that we'd have to be apart. I only hoped it wouldn't be often or for too long.

The sun had set by the time we arrived at the barn to find a truck with Colorado plates parked near the entrance. Sam and I were about to walk in when a man came out.

"Hello, can I help you?" he asked.

"This is Samantha Marquez, and I'm Beau Barrett." He tipped his hat to Sam, and he and I shook hands. "Sam has inherited the property," I said, not knowing how else to be other than direct.

His brow furrowed, and he looked from me to her. "Pardon my manners, ma'am. I'm Cord Wheaton."

When she didn't speak, I continued. "It is our understanding that you were employed by Mrs. Covert to care for her livestock."

He shifted on his feet. "Not by Mrs. Covert. I never met her. Hoss hired me."

"Hoss?" My question was as much about the name as about who he was.

"Yeah, um, his last name is Schultz. That's all I know besides that he oversees the vineyards and winery. Things have been chaotic since my uncle passed away. He and my grandfather worked for the Coverts all their lives. No one else knew what all they did."

"How long have you been here?" Sam asked.

"Since December 20. A few days after my uncle died."

"Who handled the livestock in the time in between?"

"I'm not sure about that either." Cord was clearly uncomfortable responding to our questions, given how often he shifted on his feet. Either that, or he was in need of a lavatory.

"But you've been hired, yes?"

"Hoss asked I stick around until the estate was figured out."

I pointed to his truck. "You're from Colorado?"

"Yes, sir," answered the man I doubted was any younger than me.

Sam shuddered, and I put my arm around her. "Shall we continue this conversation inside?" I motioned to the main residence.

"We could go into the barn office. There's a heater in there."

When Sam looked up at me, I nodded, and we followed Cord inside. The conversation thus far was confusing, at best. However, I sensed there was more to Mr. Wheaton than met the eye. If I had to wager a guess, I'd say he was intentionally being evasive.

He unlocked the office door, flipped on the lights, and turned on the space heater, then motioned for the two of us to take a seat. Given there were only three chairs in the room, he was left sitting behind the desk, something I also sensed he wasn't comfortable doing.

"Let's see if I can summarize." I began. "Your grandfather and uncle worked for Mrs. Covert for many years."

When he nodded, I continued.

"You said you arrived a few days after your uncle died. Had he been ill?"

"I'm not sure, sir. I guess the question, now, is whether you want me to stay on or if you want to hire someone else."

"We want you to stay on," Sam responded before I could.

Cord looked at me.

"You will be working for Ms. Marquez, so the decision is hers."

"Should I check with Mr. Schultz for the details of your employment?" she asked.

"Yes, ma'am."

"Understand that this is outside of your job and merely a personal question you do not have to answer."

"Yes, ma'am," he repeated.

Sam stood, so I did too. "How old are you, Cord?"

"Twenty-seven, ma'am."

"For the record, I'm twenty-five. Two years younger than you are. You can call me Sam."

Cord looked at me.

"Him, you still call sir."

"Yes, ma'am, err, Sam."

"Where to, ma'am?" I asked once we were in the SUV. Sam slugged me, and we both laughed.

Because we'd ordered room service from the Roycroft's dining room for lunch, we opted to have dinner in the village. This time, I chose, since she had last night.

"Irish okay?" I asked when I pulled up in front of the pub I'd overheard someone raving about on our way out of the inn earlier.

"It's perfect."

I looked over when her tone didn't quite convey the enthusiasm that went along with such a response. She was looking at her phone.

"Did you call Alex?" she asked.

"Did *I*?" I raised a brow. What was she suggesting? Did she think I would go so far as to contact her boss on her behalf?

Sam rolled her eyes. "Yes, Beau. Did *you*?"

"I did not, and I must say, I do not appreciate the implication."

While she nodded, she did not apologize. "Odd. She sent me a text asking me to check in. God, I hope she isn't thinking of opening Stave early."

"Wait. Didn't you say you weren't returning? At least not now?"

"Yes. I did say that."

"Have you changed your mind?"

"I have not."

I took a deep breath and let it out more loudly than was necessary. "This conversation is reminiscent of the one we had earlier with Cord Wheaton."

Sam put her phone down and shifted so she was facing me. "I was going to ask your opinion about him. Something isn't adding up."

"I agree. I'd say Mr. Wheaton is being evasive, and that's allowing him the benefit of the doubt."

Her eyes opened wide. "Do you think he's lying about something?"

"Only by omission. However, there is far more to his story and that of his uncle than he's saying."

"I agree. Maybe I shouldn't have said we wanted him to stay on."

"Had you asked, I would've agreed to doing so, if only in the interim."

"What do you think we should do?"

I loved that, in both instances, she'd said we rather than just I. "I think the circumstances of Cord Wheaton's arrival at the Lilacs is a mystery you and I will solve together."

17

Sam

"Hey, girl," said Alex when she answered my call.

"Hi. Is everything okay?"

"It is now. Where in the blazes are you?"

I didn't want to be rude to my boss, but why would she ask where I was? "Did something happen at Stave?" If it had, why hadn't I gotten an alert on my phone? As manager, I was listed as the first point of contact.

"Stave is fine. Mrs. Jenkins, however, believes you've been abducted by a very rich alien. I added the alien part, by the way. I'm surprised she hasn't posted missing-neighbor signs around town."

"Mrs. Jenkins?"

Alex chuckled. "She plays *Bridge* with my mom and mentioned you'd gone missing along with a handsome and seemingly wealthy man who loaded you and Wanda into, I'll quote now, 'the biggest truck she'd ever seen.' She added that you'd been gone since New Year's Eve and she's worried you've been kidnapped."

Where should I start? "First of all, she saw me four days after that when she asked me to wait to do my laundry so she could finish hers before her *Bridge* game."

"I'll be honest with you, Sam. I'm far more interested in knowing who this rich truck driver is." Alex laughed a second time. "I'm envisioning a semi parked on the street fronting your building and the driver hopping out with massive gold chains around his neck, maybe attired in Gucci. Of course, the longer I went without contacting you, the more elaborate my visions of this guy became."

I looked over at Beau, who nodded.

"It was an SUV, and while this should not be public knowledge, meaning do not repeat this to anyone…"

"I won't. Cross my heart."

Even with that, I wasn't sure I could trust Alex.

Beau motioned for me to go ahead and mouthed, "It's okay."

"I'm with Beau."

"I had a feeling." Alex went from sounding amused to concerned. "Is he okay?"

"He's fine. He just needed some time away."

"I completely get it. After my dad died, I would've crawled into a cave for weeks if Maddox would've let me. And given our relationship was a secret back then, he went to great lengths to look out for me without divulging something I didn't want anyone to know. God, I love that man." Alex sighed, and I could picture the look on her face. She had the same smile whenever she talked about her husband.

"Anyway, what wild adventure are you two off on?"

"I'm not sure you'd believe it if I told you."

"Oh, I'm liking this even more."

"Actually, Alex, I was going to call you tonight anyway. I'm, um…I need to take more time off. I know this really puts you in a bind, but—"

"Stop right there. You do whatever it is you need to do. Stave will be fine. Peyton and I can jump in, and so can our husbands." Peyton was Alex's partner in the wine bar and tasting room and was married to Alex's husband's brother. "Take all the time you need," she added.

"I…uh…"

"Go ahead and tell her," Beau urged quietly, but not enough that she didn't hear him.

"Oh my God! Are you and Beau married?"

I gasped. "*Married?* Where did you come up with that?"

"Look, everyone knows the man worships the ground you walk on, and you light up every time he comes into Stave."

I felt a flush travel from my neck up to my cheeks, and when I looked at Beau, he was smiling like the cat that ate the canary, as they say.

"Beau and I are not married. I received some unexpected news the day Mrs. Jenkins last saw me. I inherited property from a distant family member, and Beau brought me here to meet with the attorney handling the estate. We're in New York, by the way."

"New York?" she gasped the same way I had when she asked if Beau and I were married. "I can't believe he talked you into getting on a plane. Bravo, Beauregard."

"He didn't. We drove." Just the idea of willingly boarding something that weighs two hundred thousand pounds that then climbs to forty thousand feet in the air was enough to make my blood curdle more than any horror movie I'd ever seen.

"I see. So, this inheritance, what does it entail?"

Alex wasn't the type of person who hesitated to ask when there was something she wanted to know. Conversely, she expected that if someone didn't want to talk about whatever it was, they'd have the *cajones* to say so.

"A lot. A house, a barn, vineyards, a winery. I'm sure there's more, but that alone is overwhelming. Oh, and money."

"Holy Hannah! Wow! I'm so happy for you, Sam. Sad for me, but happy for you."

"Why are you sad?"

"It's a very long commute from New York, girl-friend, and that's if you fly, which we both know you will not. Anyway, do not give us another thought. What can I do on my end to make this easier for you? What about your apartment?"

"Um, I'm not quite there yet. For now, I just need a little more time. In order for me to be back to open Stave mid-month, we'd have to leave tomorrow or the next day, and there are—"

"Samantha Marquez, you know I love you, so when I say this, it comes from a place of great caring. You're fired."

I laughed out loud. "Gee, thanks, Alex."

"Keep in touch, and let me know how it's going. If you need me to, I can pack up your apartment and ship your stuff to you."

The woman stunned me on a regular basis, but this was above and beyond. "Thank you, and I will keep in touch. Right now, my plan is to return before the end of the month."

"I heard Beau in the background. Can I talk to him?"

When he nodded, I put the call on speaker. "Go ahead," I said.

"Make her stay there as long as she needs to, even if it's forever."

"I will do." Beau smiled, and the warmth and love I saw in his eyes filled me with a sense of peace. "Bye, Alex." He reached out and hit the end-call button on my phone. "Well, there you have it. You no longer have a job on the West Coast to return to."

I rolled my eyes. "You know she wasn't serious."

Beau took my hand in his. "I've known Alex a long time. As long as I've known you, in fact. And while she would give you your job back if you needed her to, she's also allowing you to explore this potential windfall entirely guilt free."

"I hate looking at it that way. Someone *died*, Beau. Someone I never knew. I don't understand why Cena made me her beneficiary, and until I do, I cannot be happy about this."

"What about looking at it from a different perspective? Yes, Cena died, but after a very long life. Less than one percent of the world's population live to be as old as she was."

I raised a brow. "Where did you come up with that statistic?"

Beau shrugged. "I looked it up. While you were snoring, by the way."

"I don't snore."

Like me, he raised a brow. "Wanda and I beg to differ. Now, let's eat." He opened his door, then came around to open mine.

"I can't get the picture of a wealthy, semi-driving alien out of my head."

He laughed. "Neither can I, and don't forget the massive gold chains."

The food and atmosphere at the pub were awesome. Like at the restaurant the night before, within an hour of being there, Beau knew all the employees by name. He also knew most of the patrons of the crowded place.

"I don't know how you do it," I said, taking a sip of the beer someone had bought for us while I went to the bathroom. "You make friends wherever you go."

"It's my good looks and charming personality."

I nodded and took another sip.

"What, no witty comeback? No remark designed to keep my already overly inflated ego in check?"

"You spoke the truth."

His head cocked. "Even the good-looks part?"

"Especially that part."

Beau put his hand on the back of my neck, leaned forward, and kissed me. "What's on your mind, my love?"

I kissed him back. "Everything. Telling Alex made this inheritance more real, somehow. Given I was already overwhelmed and still concerned this is all a mistake, the pit in my stomach has grown into a rock."

He took both my hands in his. "I will not allow this to harm you. If at any point I fear it will, I'll step in, Samantha."

"Meaning what?"

"There are a number of solutions, should this turn ugly, starting with buying the place myself to get you out from under it."

"What would that solve? And why would you if, as you said, it turned ugly?"

"As I said, there are a number of solutions. That is but one."

I folded my arms. "You didn't answer my question."

"Rather than doing so, let me tell you what I learned while you were in the loo."

"About Cena?" I hoped it was. I was certain the sooner I knew how the two of us were connected, the smaller the rock would get.

"Indirectly. According to Norman over there—who bought this round of beer, by the way—there is a fascinating history related to the Lilacs and the Covert family."

"What?"

"To begin, while we don't yet know the exact value of the investment portfolio about to become yours, my prediction is it will be worth far more than either you or I anticipated."

This wasn't helping. In fact, it was making it worse. "What does that have to do with history?" I snapped.

"This is good news, Sam."

I bristled, mainly because I knew he was right. That he was, did nothing to placate me.

"The Lilacs was originally built as a summer retreat for the Covert family."

I shook my head and laughed, but not because I found it funny. "What did their main residence look like?"

"Also according to Norman, their home in the city was over fifty thousand square feet."

"You're not serious." My apartment wasn't even five hundred.

"More about that later. The Lilacs originally housed the family's horse-breeding operation. Then they raised horses for transportation, à la horse and buggies. When automobiles cut into that market, they switched their focus to polo ponies as well as racehorses."

"Does that mean there are more horses than those we've seen?"

Beau shook his head. "In the late fifties, the family began converting the land dedicated to the breeding operation to vineyards." He looked over at me. "The significance of that particular time in history is?"

I smirked. "Vitis vinifera vines grafted with North American rootstock were refined, resulting in previously unheard of pest- and disease-resistant hybrids."

He smiled. "Precisely. Manley, it seems, had an exceptional mind for business."

"Or Cena did."

"Touché," he said, beaming at me more than smiling. "I believe you're onto something. According to what I've read, it was Cena who suggested Manley sell the city property to the Roman Catholic Diocese—probably the only entity able to afford such a purchase."

"Read? I wasn't in the restroom that long, Beau."

He held up his phone. "The internet is a marvelous thing, my love." He raised a brow and leaned forward to kiss me. "Eye-rolling remains unnecessary for the foreseeable future and beyond."

While everything Beau had told me about the Lilacs and the Coverts was fascinating, it only heightened my anxiety. I knew nothing about owning *anything*. Literally. Not a house, not property, not investments.

If it weren't for Beau, I never would've come here, let alone considered staying on longer than two days.

"Listen, there's something I want to say, and I need you to be serious for a minute," I began.

His expression sobered.

"Thank you. Without you, I wouldn't be here, and even though I'm more stressed out than I ever have been in my life, in the back of my mind, I know I really don't have to be. What you said earlier, about stepping in if things get ugly—I know you would. I knew it before you said it. I can't begin to think of ways to tell you how much I appreciate you."

"You already have done, Samantha. You've loved me despite my plethora of shortcomings. In all the years we've known each other, you have unfailingly opened your heart to me every time I've needed you."

I was about to speak, but Beau held his hand up.

"I beg you to let me finish."

"Go ahead."

"I don't know the exact moment I came to this realization, but I cannot live without you. How's that for a daunting undertaking? I'd say it far surpasses the commitment necessary to manage the Lilacs."

I waited a few seconds to see if he had more to say. When he didn't, I spoke. "I've never said this to anyone else. Not a single soul."

"Tell me," he whispered.

"I cannot live without you, either."

When both of our eyes filled with tears, Beau stood. "Come on, let's get out of here. I need to be alone with you—preferably, both of us naked."

I smiled and took his hand. We were almost to the door when we came face-to-face with Cord Wheaton, who'd just come in.

"Evenin'," he said, removing his hat.

"Hello, Cord. We were just on our way out, but can we buy you a drink?" Beau asked.

He looked beyond us to a man I hadn't noticed previously sitting at the bar. He appeared to be sneering at us. "Nah, but thanks. I don't think I'll stick around."

Beau motioned for Cord to go ahead of us, and we followed him through the door. "What was that about?" he asked once we were outside.

"Is there somewhere we can talk? Privately, I mean?"

"We could return to the Lilacs," I suggested, not knowing of anywhere else we could ensure we weren't overheard.

We agreed to meet there after I stopped by the inn to check on Wanda. "Give us twenty minutes?" I asked.

Cord nodded and walked over to his truck.

"What would you think of checking out of the inn and staying on the estate?" Beau asked.

"Now?"

He shook his head. "After we meet with Mr. Creola tomorrow."

"Can I think about it?"

"It is entirely your decision, my love. We will stay or leave the inn at your discretion."

"It would be a lot less expensive. I mean, if the house really is mine."

Beau smiled. "It's becoming more real to you, isn't it?"

While I nodded, I felt the rock in my stomach grow to the size of a boulder. Something told me everything was *not* as it seemed.

18

Beau

As I turned into the drive leading to the main residence, I reminded myself security on the property needed to be increased as soon as I could make it happen. Primarily, installing an electric gate. That would be easy. The other measures I envisioned would require I reveal my whereabouts to at least one person.

First, though, our conversation with Cord Wheaton. I'd seen the face of evil more than once in the years I'd been involved with Los Caballeros—a good-guy vigilante group per se, a bit like Robin Hood, except we didn't steal from the rich; we were the rich. Tonight, I saw it again. Whoever the man sitting at the bar was, he clearly harbored a great deal of animosity toward Cord. One might even say hatred. But why would someone feel such strong emotion over a man who'd been in the state less than a month?

Then again, perhaps this wasn't his first visit and when he was here previously, he'd made at least one enemy.

"You're deep in thought," said Sam, looking over at me.

"Lost in the mystery of Cord Wheaton and the man seated at the bar."

"He gave me the creeps, especially since there was something familiar about him—which makes zero sense."

"I'm hoping Cord will be a bit more forthcoming than he was earlier. I've no intention of interrogating him. He obviously knew the man and was discomfited enough to choose to leave the bar. Either he shares why, or I suggest you consider replacing him."

Sam breathed in deeply when we saw the truck with Colorado plates parked near the main residence. She let it out slowly and waited after I parked for me to come around and open her door.

Once the three of us were inside the house, I suggested he and Sam sit in the same room where we met with the attorney while I went into the kitchen to see if I could find anything to drink. Given there was a winery on the property, I hoped there would be wine at least.

"Success!" I said to myself when I found a red blend along with glasses. As far as other booze, I hadn't come across any.

I joined them and held up the bottle. "Cord, are you a wine drinker?" I noticed he'd removed his cowboy hat and had set it on a table near the front door.

"I am, thanks."

I suppose it didn't speak well of me that I'd assumed he would've preferred beer or something stronger. "Where shall we begin?" I asked once each of us held a beverage and I'd taken a seat beside Sam on the sofa.

Cord set his glass on the table in front of him and momentarily leaned forward with his elbows on his knees before sitting upright again. "What I'm about to tell you is going to sound crazy."

Sam chuckled. "No crazier than my story."

Cord smiled. It was the first time I'd seen him do so. "Guess you're right, ma'am, I mean, Sam. Now, I sound like Dr. Seuss."

We laughed, but Cord's expression quickly changed to a scowl, and he shook his head. "My father passed away last year."

I offered our condolences.

"Thanks, but I doubt my siblings are any sorrier than I am that he's gone. The man was a mean *sonuvabitch*."

His comment was reminiscent of Henry Allen saying the same thing about Cena's husband, Manley. "Go on," I prompted.

"You'd think death would've put an end to the way the old man manipulated my brothers, sister, and me, but it sure as hell didn't. In fact, it got worse." He looked at Sam. "Sorry for my language."

"No apology necessary, Cord. You'll hear plenty of swear words from Beau." She nudged me, and I turned to kiss her cheek.

"Anyway, our family owns ranchland in Crested Butte, Colorado, called the Roaring Fork. It's been operating at a loss for a few years, not unlike other ranches in the area, but that isn't the point. In order for his beneficiaries to inherit, my father had stipulations. The first was that my oldest brother had to remain on the property for a full year. Buck left Colorado when he turned eighteen, swearing he'd never come back. He worked for the CIA for a while, then went into private intelligence."

Buck Wheaton—the name sounded vaguely famil-iar. I'd add it to the list of people to look into I'd begun mentally preparing.

"Given what he does for a living, the requirement posed a significant hardship for him since he couldn't be away for longer than forty-eight hours."

"What would happen if he didn't comply?" I asked.

"We'd lose everything. The terms of the trust were if Buck didn't do as Dad demanded, all assets were to be sold and given to charity." He raked his hair with his fingers. "Ol' Buck did what he had to, and while we all expected him to leave the minute he could, he and his wife settled there instead. Given that's what our father wanted all along, I guess he got his wish."

I had no idea what this had to do with the man at the pub, but the story was fascinating in itself. "Go on," I repeated.

"We thought everything would be said and done with the inheritance when we returned to the lawyer's office, but that's when we learned there was more. As I said, Buck was first. I was next."

"What does that mean?" Sam asked.

"That's why I'm here. Actually, that's what got me here. The why is a mystery."

"Quite conveniently timed, given your uncle had just passed away," I commented.

"I think that was coincidental. All the trust said was I was supposed to travel to East Aurora, New York—a place I'd never heard of—and get a job at the Lilacs. And, like my brother, I have to remain here a full year."

My eyes met Sam's, and I wondered if she was thinking the same thing I was. Had Cena had a hand in this? If so, what was Cord's connection to her?

"I hate to disrespect the dead, but I guess it's a good thing my uncle died when he did. I'm not sure I would've been hired on otherwise."

"You don't think your uncle would've given you a job, considering the trust's stipulations?" I asked.

Cord shook his head and scrubbed his face. "He didn't know me from Adam, sir."

"Was he your father's brother?"

"No. My mother's, and until that day in the lawyer's office, no one in our family knew she had any siblings."

"An hour ago, I would've said Cena Covert leaving everything to me was the most bizarre thing I'd ever heard, but, Cord, I think you've got me beat."

He smiled. "Not a distinction I desire."

"Believe me, I understand."

"What about the man who hired you? Hoss Schultz?" I asked.

"Yes, sir."

"Does he know anything?"

"He says he doesn't, and that's why he asked me to stick around until the estate was figured out." He looked between us again. "Have you met him yet?"

"We have not," I responded.

"I have no reason for thinking this other than my gut saying I should, but I have a feeling Hoss may have expected someone else would inherit."

"Who did he think would?" Sam asked.

"I have no idea except, that man you saw at the bar? The one who was throwin' daggers at me?"

"Yes?" I asked.

"It wasn't the first time I've seen him."

"Where else have you run into him?"

"Here. Talkin' to Hoss."

My earlier desire to implement security measures on the property intensified. Until it was in place, I wouldn't feel comfortable suggesting Sam stay here.

"Would you both excuse me?" I asked, standing.

"Of course," Sam responded, but I saw curiosity in her eyes.

"I need to make a quick call." Two, actually, but it wasn't necessary I be that specific. "I'll only be a moment or two," I murmured, leaning over for a kiss.

Rather than return to the kitchen, I went exploring. Neither Sam nor I had taken the time to look at the house, which was quite large, even by my family's standards. On the other hand, compared to the Coverts' former home in the city, this residence would be considered small at only fourteen thousand square feet.

After stumbling on a second-story sitting room similar to the one downstairs, I closed the door and retrieved my mobile.

"Hey, Beau," my best mate, Cru Avila, said when he answered my call.

One of the reasons I considered him such was evident in his greeting. If I felt compelled to share information, that was one thing, but Cru would never ask questions. "I'm in need of help, my friend."

"What can I do?" he responded.

"Call a meeting of Los Caballeros at your earliest convenience. I'm looking for background information on several people." It occurred to me I should've attempted to take a snapshot of the man at the pub. However, it was doubtful I would've been successful without him seeing me do it. Instead, I asked Cru to see if one of the *caballeros* could get their hands on the bar's security footage. The place was big enough I didn't doubt they'd have it.

Requesting assistance meant I had to share my whereabouts, not that I'd wanted to keep it a secret. It was more that I wanted time on my own. If there was anyone in particular I wasn't anxious to learn where I was, it was my older brother. I'd not ask Cru to keep it from him, though. It wouldn't be fair.

How Sam was involved was different. Before divulging any of it, I asked Cru to keep the specifics of it to himself as much as possible. When he agreed, I told him what was in the package she'd received via courier last week.

"Holy shit," he said when I explained about the inheritance. "She has no idea who this woman is?"

"None whatsoever. The mystery deepened tonight, in fact, and relates to a man named Cord Wheaton. He's on the list of those I'll forward for the *caballeros* to look into."

"You got it, Beau. Anything else?"

"My next call is to Burns Butler. I was stunned to see the lack of security at an estate so large."

"Think you'll need a crew?"

He and I both chuckled at his use of the homophone.

"I'm sure I will now that you've made the suggestion."

"Who *don't* you want to come with me?"

"I think you know the answer, my friend, not that Press would be available to do so."

"Let me know what Burns has to say and if you want me to go over and talk to him."

Given the Butlers' and Avilas' properties were adjacent, it wouldn't be a hardship for him. "It's likely I will. Much appreciated, Cru."

Thankfully, my call with Burns was brief, given I was anxious to return downstairs. He immediately agreed it would make the most sense for Cru and him to meet in person this evening. It was more than I'd expected and said so.

"Samantha is one of our own, Beau," he said as if that was the only explanation necessary.

"Again, many thanks."

We rang off, and I made my way downstairs, greatly relieved at how much I'd been able to put in motion. When I reached the bottom step, I could hear Sam and Cord laughing. My shoulders immediately tensed. It was preposterous for me to be jealous of a man we'd both just met; however, the shift in my relationship with her was new. And as she and I had already established, I could be an insecure bastard. Most times, I hid it fairly well. I couldn't hide anything from Samantha, though, and for that, I was glad.

No one knew me the same way she did. I'd never once felt uncomfortable about being vulnerable when I was with her. I believed the same was true in reverse. Case in point, *I* was the person she'd called when she received the package from the attorney.

I was also the person who'd spent hours making love with her. Once we were alone tonight, I had no doubt we'd spend hours more. While all the arguments I made with myself were sound, my jaw still clenched when I walked in and saw her smiling at Cord.

She looked up at me and patted the cushion where I'd sat previously. I took a seat and put my arm around her shoulders.

"Everything okay?" she asked.

"Yes. We'll chat later."

Sam nodded.

"We'll be meeting with the estate's attorney sometime tomorrow. We'll also make it a point to introduce ourselves to Mr. Schultz."

Cord nodded like Sam had. "Let me know if there's anything I can do to help." He scrubbed his face a second time. "I know this is a lot to ask, especially since we've just met, but if there's any way I can stay on here, I'd appreciate the opportunity."

"Of course," I said. No doubt, he knew Sam keeping him on was dependent on many things, none of which we could determine tonight.

When I stood, Cord did as well. He said good night to Sam, and I walked him to the door.

"I guess I don't need to warn you to be mindful what you say to Hoss," he said.

"You do not."

He grabbed his hat and walked out the front door.

"Things are getting weirder," Sam said when I returned.

"Agreed. About our conversation earlier, when I asked how you'd feel about relocating from the inn here, I'd like to hold off doing so for now."

"You called Burns, didn't you?" While the man's expertise in security and technology wasn't exactly public knowledge, working for Alex Butler, who was married to Burns' son, she was likely privy to more than most.

I grinned. "I did, and his response when I asked for help with security was, 'Samantha is one of our own.'"

Her eyes filled with tears, and one ran down her cheek. I brushed it away with the pad of my thumb.

"They say you don't know who your real friends are until you need them. I certainly have learned who mine are. Starting with you."

"I'd say what we learned is our feelings go beyond friendship. I love you, Samantha."

She leaned up and kissed me. "I love you, Beau."

"What do you say we check on Wanda?"

"I'd say you're a good cat dad."

Was it crazy that I found myself wanting to be more than a father to a feline? I'd never thought much about having a family in the past. Now, I longed for just that with her. Not only starting a family. I wanted to marry Samantha Marquez. Sadly, if I told her so, I doubted she'd believe me.

19

Sam

Listening to Beau talk to Mr. Creola the following morning made me realize again how lost I'd be without him. For one, I probably would've ignored the letter the attorney sent or at least procrastinated long enough that it seemed like I was ignoring it.

I studied him while he spoke, not listening to what he was saying as much as wondering if this thing between us would last. Yes, Beau had told me he was in love with me, but in the back of my mind, I still wasn't sure he knew what that meant. Or if I did.

How long would it be before he got bored? Or realize I didn't have the allure he thought I did? And what about the things in his life he was neglecting because he was with me?

He oversaw the vineyards at his parents' estate, where their wine business generated millions of dollars each year. He couldn't just walk away from that. Yes, this was the slowest time of the year for him, but what about when the growing season got underway? He couldn't turn his back on it to help me.

The idea that he'd leave, no matter how much he'd assured me he wouldn't, was like a bucket of cold water dumped over my head. If I was going to accept this inheritance, I had to figure out how to manage it on my own. I couldn't sit back and passively let Beau take over. I had to learn to do this like I'd had to do with everything else in my life.

My degree was in agricultural business, and while that hadn't taught me how to run an estate like Cena's, there were certain parts of it I could handle. Like the vineyards and winery. Maybe not right away, but if Beau was able to stick around long enough to mentor me, I felt confident I'd learn enough to eventually run things myself.

When I heard Beau mention the contract between Lilac Lane and the Schultz winery, I sat up straighter. "Do you have a copy of it?" I asked.

My cheeks flushed when Mr. Creola said it was included in the packet he'd sent to me.

"Yes, but do you have one here?" I asked.

"Of course," he responded, shuffling through the contents of a folder. "Here it is." He handed it to me.

I read through it and looked at him with wide eyes. "This says the contract was signed two years ago and extends another eight."

"That's right."

"It doesn't make sense that Cena would sign a ten-year contract when she was ninety-eight years old."

"May I take a look?" Beau asked.

I handed it to him.

"Who is James Rooker?" he asked.

"He was the livestock manager at the Lilacs. Where do you see the name?" asked Mr. Creola.

Beau set the contract on the desk. "Here," he said, pointing. I leaned forward and saw the man had signed the document on Cena's behalf.

"My apologies. With the vast extent of the estate, I missed that in my review. You should also know our firm did not handle the negotiation between Mrs. Covert and Schultz Wineries."

"Can I see that again, please?" I asked.

Beau plucked the paper from the desk and handed it back to me.

"It doesn't list a firm, but the signature was notarized." I read through it a second time. There was no mention of Cena naming anyone, let alone James

Rooker, as having authority to negotiate or sign on her behalf.

"Did Mrs. Covert have a power of attorney in place, granting James Rooker the authority to do this?" Beau asked.

"To my knowledge, she did not."

"Then how can it be valid?" I asked.

"There's one other thing I want to take a look at," Beau said, and I handed him the contract. "Good Lord," he muttered. "What Schultz is being paid is astronomical." He stared at the attorney. "How long have you represented Mrs. Covert?"

"She engaged the firm eighteen months ago when she revised the trust."

"Who did prior?" Beau asked.

"Gerald Sokolowski. He was independent, meaning not affiliated with a firm."

"Do you have his contact information?" I asked.

"Mr. Sokolowski passed away six months before Mrs. Covert came to us."

"Let me piece this together. The contract between Cena Covert of Lilac Lane Winery and Schultz Wineries was drafted two years ago, signed by someone it appears did not have the authority to do so. On top of that, the attorney who most likely drafted it, passed away weeks later?"

"As it appears, sir," Mr. Creola responded.

"Are all of Mrs. Covert's assets included in the trust?" he asked.

"To the best of my knowledge. As it relates to this conversation, I can assure you Lilac Lane Winery most definitely is."

"Would you excuse us for a moment?" Beau asked.

The attorney agreed and left us alone in his office.

"The reason I asked him to step out is because, as I predicted, this is about to turn ugly, my love."

"I agree."

His eyes bored into mine. "Tell me what you're thinking."

I couldn't now, not here. "Let's talk once we leave."

He nodded and stood, holding his hand out to me. "Let's go."

"Are we finished with Mr. Creola?" I asked.

"For now."

"Coincidences abound," he said once we were in the SUV.

"Cena's attorney dies. Then Cord's uncle. Then Cena herself."

Beau's jaw was tight. "I'm beginning to think there's something rotten in the state of Denmark, as they say."

The feeling of dread in my stomach intensified. "Do you suspect foul play?"

Beau reached over and took my hand. "Not yet, particularly with Cena. However, I'm sure you'll agree that all is not on the up-and-up."

"I do."

"What were you thinking earlier?"

I couldn't lie to Beau, even knowing the answer would hurt him.

"Whatever it is, just say it."

I turned to face him. "A few minutes into the meeting, I wondered if, once you have to leave, I can manage this on my own."

Hurt flashed in his eyes, but he quickly masked it. "And now?"

"This is all too much for me, Beau. Even if everything was on the up-and-up, as you said, it's too much."

"I have another question."

I took a deep breath, anticipating what he was about to say.

"Why did you say 'once I had to leave'?"

When I tried to remove my hand, he held on tighter.

"You have a life, Beau, and it isn't here."

His jaw clenched. "The hell, it's not."

"What about Barrett Family Estates?"

"I can assure you my father and brother are perfectly capable of hiring someone to assume my responsibilities. In fact, the pool of qualified candidates is vastly greater in Napa Valley than it is here." He leaned in closer. "Tell me what precipitated these thoughts."

As I figured would happen, my eyes filled with tears.

Beau dropped my hands and leaned against his seat. "Let me guess. You've convinced yourself what I feel for you isn't real. Either that, or you think it won't last," he snapped.

"Don't be mad at me. I've seen it happen before. I can't help but think—"

"Wrong, Samantha. You *can* help but think I would leave you, given I have professed my love many times now. What's more, you said you love me too."

"But—"

"I'm not finished."

I couldn't remember another time when Beau had raised his voice to me like he did now.

"Whatever assurances you need, I will give to you. I've told you I won't leave. Multiple times, in fact. I've also just told you, in so many words, that my life *is* here." He closed his eyes, then reopened them slowly. "Last night, I—" His voice broke, and he cleared his throat. "You told me I was a good cat dad. Would you like to know where my mind went?"

I nodded.

"Bloody hell, this is not the way I wanted to do this."

"Do what?" I managed to say even though I was on the verge of sobbing. Was he ending things between us already? Over a joke about my cat?

He faced me and took both my hands in his. "I want to be more than a cat dad. I want to be a father to *our* children, Samantha. What's more, I want to marry you. Today, if I believed for one minute you'd have me."

"What?" I gasped.

"You heard me. I want to marry you and fill that big house that's about to become yours with as many children as I can convince you to bear."

I attempted blinking away my tears, but there were too many falling down my cheeks.

"How does that make you feel, Sam? Terrified?"

I shook my head. "Not terrified."

"What, then?"

"I'm not sure."

"Samantha." When his voice cracked again, I ached for him. "Don't push me away. I beg you."

"I won't."

He squeezed my fingers. "Do you promise?"

"I do." It wasn't hard for me to make the vow. I worried more that Beau had gotten caught up in this thing between us and would eventually realize his feelings weren't as strong as he thought. Then it would be me who'd get pushed away. God knew what I'd do when it happened.

His cell phone rang. "Forgive me, but I must take this."

"Go ahead," I responded when I realized he was waiting for me to.

He let go of my hands and faced forward. "Cru, what have you got for me?" Beau paused for several seconds. "That's excellent. We'll see you this evening, then. Give my thanks to Burns."

He ended the call and turned back toward me. "Cru, Snapper, and Kick will be arriving tonight. Another man, Decker Ashford, and his team will be traveling with them. They will implement a security protocol at the Lilacs. We'll begin with the basics, like constructing an electronic gate and securing the main residence. The system will grow quickly from there."

I was too stunned to know what to say.

"What I'd like to do now more than anything—not just want, what I feel we both need—is to return to the inn and spend the rest of the day making love."

God, I wanted that too. "Shouldn't we try to meet with Hoss first?"

"You're right. We must."

"After that, we can spend the rest of the day in bed."

Beau smiled, leaned forward, put his hand on the back of my neck, and kissed me like he had the first time. Then and now, it ignited my desire for him.

"Ah, I see you didn't say that just to make me feel better." He brushed my nipple with the back of his hand. "You're definitely on board. Perhaps we do have time now. After all, we need to check on Wanda."

"Yes. Wanda." While I had trouble communicating a few minutes ago, it was because I was crying too hard. Now, it was lust clouding my ability to say more than two words.

"Oh, Samantha, all the things I want to do to you…"

20

Beau

I'd said too much. Tipped my hand, as they say. Confessed that not only did I want to marry Sam, but I wanted to have as many children as we could. Surprisingly, she hadn't flinched. Or at least she'd said she wasn't terrified.

I thanked God she'd agreed to return to the inn with me rather than seek out this Hoss character. I *needed* to be close to her. Bodies connected. Skin on skin. I needed to hear my name on her lips as she cried out in pleasure and hear her tell me again that she loved me.

The drive from the Lilacs to the inn, then taking the lift to our floor, even the walk to the room, felt endless.

I told Sam I'd tend to Wanda. Rather than demanding she wait for me naked and on the bed, then changing my mind like I had before, I left it up to her.

After I fed the cat and opened one of the catnip-filled toys I'd gotten for her what felt like weeks rather than days ago, I made my way to the bedroom. I smiled when I saw the door was closed. My mouth salivated at what waited for me on the other side.

"Knock, knock," I said, rapping lightly.

"Come in, my love," she said, using the term of endearment I used for her.

I opened the door and found her lying on the bed, wearing a silk wrap I'd not seen before. Its deep red hue, the color of a rich Cabernet Sauvignon, against her olive skin was breathtaking.

"Samantha, you are magnificent," I said with bated breath, marveling at her beauty as I stalked toward her. I was within a step or two when she shifted and the wrap fell open, revealing her breasts.

Too impatient to remove my clothes, I toed off my boots, climbed on the bed, and spread her legs so I could rest between them. I began at the hollow of her neck, kissing my way down the soft skin of her sternum, then gently sucked her pink nipple into my mouth.

Sam's mewls of pleasure nearly undid me as she weaved her fingers in my hair, holding me to her breast. I couldn't stop there, though. My lips and fingers trailed down her body until I reached the hot, wet heaven between her thighs.

"Beau," she cried when I stroked between her folds first with my finger, then my tongue.

"Yes, my love?"

She reached for the button on my trousers, but I caught her wrist.

"I am too on edge, my gorgeous Samantha. If I allow you to touch me now, the pleasure I'd otherwise give you will have to wait."

She stuck out her bottom lip, and I caught it between my teeth, gently pinching her nipple at the same time I ground my hardness between her legs.

"Do you feel how much I want you? How much I need you?"

"Please, Beau."

"Please? What is it you need?"

"Your skin on mine." Given she'd said something so close to my earlier thoughts, I couldn't deny her. I stood, pushing her legs open when she moved to close them.

"Let me look at you." I pulled at the buttons on my shirt, not caring if every one popped off and scattered on the floor. Her eyes trailed from my face to the ink on my chest. "Like this?" My finger outlined the petals of the flower that transformed into the sun.

"Not as much as this." She sat on the edge of the bed, and like my finger had trailed the petal, she used hers to trace the words below my navel. "*La petite mort*," she murmured before wrapping her arms around me and pressing herself against my body so my cock was wedged between her breasts. Then she used her tongue to trace the same words she'd said aloud.

Knowing if her tongue made contact with my cock, I'd never last, I picked her up and gently rested her on the bed. I spread her legs again and pressed my finger inside her wetness. When I added a second, her breathing registered as gasps of pleasure.

"Please, Beau," she said again.

I removed my fingers but quickly replaced them with my cock, entering her slowly, waiting as her body softened and I could ease in deeper. Then I hooked one of her legs with my arm and thrust hard.

Her eyes widened. "God, Beau."

"Tell me if I hurt you."

Her head moved from side to side. "I need more."

I pulled out and thrust again, no longer able to hold myself back. I reached between our bodies and stroked her clit. "You are mine, Samantha," I groaned as her body clenched, and we reached the pinnacle of pleasure together. I kissed her, not wanting to let her go. Only then, as my breathing settled, did I realize I hadn't worn a condom.

Propping myself up with one arm, I looked into her eyes. "Sam—"

She put her finger on my lips, silencing me. "I know," she whispered.

"I've never—"

"I know that too."

"I love you."

She smiled. "I love you."

"Marry me," I blurted in what was the least romantic proposal ever uttered.

"Beau—"

I put my finger on her lips like she had mine. "Don't answer. I'll continue asking until you say yes. Otherwise, don't tell me." As much as I'd rather remain inside her forever, I eased my body from hers and rested next to her with my head on her chest.

Sam stroked my hair with one hand and tickled my forearm with the other.

"If you keep that up, I'll fall asleep, and that is the last thing I want to do."

She sighed. "I suppose we have to leave."

"Not yet, my love."

I woke with a start when I heard my mobile ringing. It was somewhere in the room, but I had no idea where. I'd ignore it, but given Cru, Snapper, and Kick were on their way, I needed to answer.

"I'm sorry," I whispered, hating that when I moved to find it, our skin would no longer touch.

The ringing stopped, then seconds later, began again.

When I reached under my trousers and found it, I groaned, recognizing the attorney's number. Why was he calling when we'd left his office a short time ago?

"Mr. Creola, what can I do for you?"

"I was able to reach Attorney Sokolowski's son. Apparently, he's taken over his father's practice. I have his contact information if you'd like it."

"Please," I responded, walking to the other room, where I remembered seeing a notepad and pen. "Go ahead."

"His name is Gerald Sokolowski Jr., and his offices are on Main Street."

I thanked him after he gave me the man's phone number, and ended the call.

"What did Mr. Creola want?" Sam asked.

"Cena's dead attorney's records may be resurfacing by way of his son. He suggested contacting him to schedule a meeting."

"We should do that prior to meeting Hoss Schultz."

I agreed and said so. Plus, I anticipated hearing from Cru saying he and the other guys had landed. "There's something we should discuss before we schedule any further meetings."

Sam was already sitting up and had covered herself with the sheet. I sat beside her on the bed. "There comes a time in the life of every *caballero* when he meets the one woman he knows he trusts without question."

Her eyes opened wide. "Beau—"

I cupped the back of her neck, leaned forward, and rested my forehead against hers. "There are things you may hear, Samantha. Other things you will be told explicitly not to share outside of what is happening at the Lilacs. I trust you, and more, I will not hide what is occurring from you, particularly since it is your property in question. Do you understand?"

"I do."

I sat upright and gazed at her. "I suppose you haven't changed your mind about…"

Sam rolled her eyes and kissed me. "You can't ask me every hour, Beau."

"First of all, it's been more than an hour—I think. Secondly, I didn't ask this time."

"Asking if I've changed my mind counts as asking."

"So, it's a no, is it?"

She pushed past me and went in to take a shower, laughing all the way.

"You're not being kind," I called after her.

She stuck her head in the door. "Beau?"

"Yes?" I grumbled.

"I love you."

I waited until I heard the bathroom door close before responding. "If you really loved me, you'd marry me." Yes, I was petulant—a fact my beloved Samantha knew well.

"If only you were still around, Mum. No one would be happier about this than you," I muttered, looking up at the sky before ringing Gerald Sokolowski Jr.

21

Sam

Warm water cascaded over my shoulders, releasing some of the tension that had settled there. None of it came from Beau. He eased my anxiety, made me feel safe and loved. But marriage? That would take a whole different level of trust.

I'd witnessed happy ones with Alex and Peyton and their husbands, as well as other couples I'd met while living in Cambria all my life, but as far as up close and personal, I had no role models for what being married to someone looked like on a daily basis.

My mother hadn't married. She didn't even know who my biological father was. Her mother had died before I was born, and I knew nothing whatsoever about my grandmother's life or who my grandfather was.

I loved her name, though—Pilar. When I was growing up, there were many times when I'd wished my mom named me after her mom instead of Samantha. Mainly because of the endless teasing I'd endured because of all the words that rhymed with Sam—spam, ham, clam, jam, yam. I'd been called them all, plus a lot more.

To me, Pilar sounded gracious and beautiful, even elegant. I remembered realizing my grandmother was the same age as Manley Jr. How crazy was it to think Cena had outlived both of them. God, I would've loved to meet her. Both Cena and Pilar, actually. I had a feeling the stories each would tell of their lives would be fascinating.

While I doubted I'd ever learn anything about my mom's mom, maybe once I had the chance to explore Cena's house, I'd find out more about her.

As I lathered shampoo in my hair, I recalled Beau's comment about her husband's business acumen. I'd half jokingly suggested it was Cena who'd thought of replacing the horse-breeding operation with grape-growing. Considering the timing of the conversion, I wondered when Manley Sr. died. Their son and daughter too. Tomorrow, I needed to remember to call St. John's Lutheran Church and ask the secretary what she could tell me about the family.

When I saw Cena's daughter Blanche's photo sitting on the piano, I'd been stunned by how much she looked like me at that same age. The attorney, Mr. Creola, said there were more pictures of Blanche throughout the house. I hoped I would have time to explore it.

That the house would soon be mine—which I still had a hard time wrapping my head around—filled me with something I'd never felt before. *Belonging.*

By and large, the community in Cambria was afflu-ent. While people like Beau and his family, Alex and hers, had always been kind to my mom and me, we'd never been part of their inner circle. We worked for them; we weren't their peers.

Now, I'd have people working for me. Not just as their boss, like at Stave, but as their employer. One more thing to boggle my mind.

I wished I could get over the feeling that as soon as I accepted this would be my life, the rug would be pulled out from under me.

The door opened, and I quickly rinsed the shampoo from my hair.

"May I join you?" Beau asked.

"Of course."

"I'm not crowding you, am I?"

"I like it," I said, wrapping my arms around him and pivoting our bodies so he was under the showerhead.

"Have I told you how much I love feeling your naked body next to mine?"

"God, Beau," I groaned when he reached around, cupped the cheeks of my bottom, and I felt his hardness press against me. "I will never get enough of you."

He pulled back and put his finger on the bottom of my chin, raising my face. "Do you mean it?"

I understood why he asked. We both felt insecure, doubtful, maybe even disbelieving. He needed my reassurance as much as I needed his. "I do, Beau. Every word."

When he kissed me, I felt everything—desire, love, relief, appreciation, acceptance, and peace. Beau and I belonged together. If there was any one thing in life I was sure of, it was that. I wasn't ready to tell him I'd marry him, but I wasn't as far away as I thought I'd be.

"I need to be inside you." His voice was thick with the same need I felt.

He lifted me, and I wrapped my legs around him at the same moment I felt him join our bodies together. I clung to his shoulders as he raised and lowered me onto his hardness. In what felt like minutes, we'd both climaxed, but he didn't let me go. He held me in his arms, and we kissed.

When he finally released me and I slid down his body, Beau was studying me. "We need to talk about my neglectfulness in using a condom."

"It's been a really long time since I've been with anyone else, Beau. Even then, we used protection."

His shoulders tensed, and he brought his forehead to mine like he'd done so often in the last few days. "You need never tell me about other *men* again."

"It's the same for me. I don't want to know anything at all about the other women in your life."

"Agreed. Now, what about birth control? I've already told you I want to have children with you, so I'm more concerned about what you want, or don't want, as it were."

"I get a shot every three months."

"Then, I'll stop worrying about it, or should I be more responsible?"

"It isn't just you, Beau. I got caught up in the moment too. But I think we should both stop worrying about it."

"How I wish we could have more uninterrupted time together," Beau said as we finished our shower then stepped out of the small enclosure. "And that Cena's house has much larger bathrooms."

"Me too. On both counts."

"By the way, we have an appointment with the attorney, Sokolowski Jr., in one hour. I also sent a message to Mr. Schultz, requesting he make himself available to meet later this afternoon."

"You've been busy."

Beau leaned forward and kissed the tip of my nose. "You were in the shower a long time."

I wasn't sure what I expected when we arrived at the attorney's office, but it wasn't the chaos we were looking at.

The man, who appeared to be close to my age, stepped around the desk in the one-room office when we walked in the open door.

"Hey, I'm Gerry. Most call me Chip, though."

"Beau Barrett, and this is Samantha Marquez."

Chip shook my hand, then Beau's. "Welcome, and sorry about the mess. My dad was, what's the word? A bit of a hoarder?"

A bit? I thought but didn't say.

"How did he ever find anything?" said Beau, shaking his head.

I smiled, glad he was never afraid to speak his mind.

"Yeah, I don't know. I'm, um, trying to get out from under it now. That's why I haven't hung out my shingle, as they say."

Beau cocked his head. "Shingle?"

"An expression for starting a practice after passing the bar."

"Ah, I see," he murmured.

"What can I do for you?" Chip asked.

"Is there somewhere we could sit and chat privately?"

I smiled again. The keyword in Beau's request was "sit," given the office chairs were piled high with files and other stuff.

"Sure, uh, there's a conference room. Let me just find a notepad."

I spotted one and pointed.

"Right. Thanks."

We followed him down the hall, where I was relieved to see the tables and chairs in the room weren't being used for storage.

"This is a common area the tenants share," Chip explained, almost as if he'd read my thoughts.

Beau pulled my chair out, then sat beside me.

"Mr. Sokolowski—"

"Please, call me Chip."

"Right. Chip. Ms. Marquez has recently learned she is the beneficiary of a trust. The woman who named her as such, Mrs. Cena Covert, passed away in December. It is our understanding your father represented Mrs. Covert, although he did not prepare said trust."

Chip's friendly demeanor shifted. He leaned forward and rested his elbows on the table. "I'm going to be completely honest with you."

My eyes opened wide. Where was this going?

"Please continue," said Beau.

"I probably shouldn't tell you this, but to be fair, I'm going to anyway as long as you agree that it remain off-the-record."

I was holding my breath and wondered if Beau was too.

"We'll agree," Beau responded. When Chip looked at me, I nodded.

"One of the reasons I haven't announced my intent to practice is that there were questionable things found in my father's files."

"Since you brought it up," Beau turned to me. "Perhaps you'd like to explain, since this is your inheritance." By the way he said it, I knew he was asking more than suggesting.

"I would." I cleared my throat. "When we met with Mr. Creola, the attorney representing the estate, yesterday, we found a contract we believe was drawn up by your father."

"For?"

"It's between Lilac Lane Winery and Schultz Wineries."

Chip sat back in his chair and steepled his fingers. "What is the issue?"

"The contract was signed by a James Rooker, but nothing in it that says Mrs. Covert gave him the authority to do so." I looked over at Beau, who nodded.

"What we're wondering, Chip, is if there was a power of attorney in place and if there were circumstances under which it was invoked."

"We can handle this one of two ways."

My eyes opened wide at Chip's response.

"Go on," said Beau.

"Again, I can give you my off-the-record opinion, or I can see if I can find the answers in my father's files."

"Given how long that might take, we'll hear your opinion."

The man rubbed the back of his neck, then looked down at the table and groaned. "As hard as this is for me to say, let alone think, I have reason to believe my dad didn't always cross his t's and dot his i's, if you know what I mean."

"Do you have reason to believe the contract might be invalid?" I asked.

"If it were me, I'd ask for proof it *is* valid."

"Anything else?" Beau turned to me and asked.

"Not that I can think of."

He stood and helped me with my chair.

"Chip, you're a good man. I hope you do start your own firm and you are very successful at it."

"I appreciate it." Chip got up too and shook both of our hands again before we left.

"It's never an easy decision when faced with honesty over loyalty," Beau said once we were in the SUV. "There's reason to admire both, I suppose."

"I liked him. I think he'll make a good attorney."

"I would say the same. In fact, you might consider asking him to be yours."

"What do we do about Mr. Schultz?" I asked.

"Wait for backup."

22

Beau

While I hadn't wanted to alarm Sam, two things made me respond as I had. First, the amount of money Schultz Wineries would lose if the contract was proven invalid. Second, the way the man at the pub had looked at us last night, the one Cord said he'd seen speaking with Hoss. I was convinced his venom was directed at all three of us rather than Cord alone.

Above all, I would not risk Sam's safety. Before starting the engine, I rang Cru.

"I was just about to call you," he said, chuckling.

"How far out are you?"

"Fifteen minutes, tops."

"Has everyone arrived?"

"Affirmative. We're caravanning. Change of plans?"

"Not at all. We'll meet at the Lilacs."

"Copy that."

"We should stop by the inn first," I said to Sam, who was staring out the passenger side window.

"Okay," she murmured.

"Everything all right?" I asked when she didn't turn to look at me.

"Is this what it's like, being rich? You have to put up gates so no one can get in? Security systems on your house? You have to worry about people trying to rip you off all the time?"

I thought about her questions for several seconds before responding. "I suppose in some ways. Let me ask you this: when you moved into your apartment, did we not purchase and install several additional locking mechanisms for your entry door?"

"We did."

"What about Stave, does it have an alarm system?"

"It does."

"And the Olallieberry Diner?"

"Yes, and I see your point."

"Sadly, there are people in the world who believe they are entitled to what others have worked very hard for." I'd never considered wanting to the make the world a better place for someone. I did for Sam. I suppose parents felt that way too. I know I would if she and I had kids. I glanced over at her. *When* we had kids.

I couldn't accept anything else besides a life with Sam. If we couldn't conceive, we'd adopt.

She sighed. "You're right."

"I'll make you a promise."

She looked over at me and smiled.

"I will always keep you safe, Samantha."

"I know you will, Beau."

"We'll just be a minute or two," I told Grayson, the valet, when I pulled up to the inn and got out. He and the other guys who worked at the inn had grown accustomed to me getting Sam's door and ceased attempting to beat me to it.

I grasped the handle to open it for her when something caught my eye. A man ducked inside and out of sight quickly, but not before I got a good enough look at him to recognize he was the same one we'd seen seated at the bar in the pub.

"How do you feel about cats?" I asked Grayson.

"I have one."

I motioned him closer and handed him a fifty and the room key. "There's a carrier near the door, and you'll see treats on the table. Use those to coax her into the carrier."

"Anything else?"

"Toss a couple of the toys lying about in with her. Oh, and her name is Wanda."

"You got it. Be right back."

I motioned for Sam to wait a moment and returned to the driver's side.

"Did you see him?" she asked when I got in.

"I did, and I asked Grayson to fetch Wanda. He'll just be a minute. Then we'll be on our way."

"He looked right at me."

As she said the words, Grayson came out the main door. I opened the back hatch, and he set the carrier inside. I thanked him, he closed the hatch, and I pulled out.

"I'm going to talk to the guys about relocating."

"Okay." Sam's arms were folded, and she nodded, but otherwise, she didn't speak again on the way to the Lilacs.

When I pulled into the drive, I saw two black SUVs near the main house. Several men, including Cord, were standing outside the vehicles.

"There she is," said Cru, coming over to hug Sam once I'd opened her door. Following him were Snapper and Kick. The three men were Alex's younger brothers, so she knew them well.

"Decker," I said, walking over to shake his hand. "I appreciate you making the trip."

"Hey, Beau. Burns doesn't ask favors very often, so when he does, I'm happy to oblige."

In intelligence security and technology, Burns Butler and Decker Ashford were considered the number one and two experts in the world. Ashford would always concede to Burns, who'd mentored him. However, Burns was likely to say Deck was the top gun.

"I was surprised to see ol' Cord here," he said, motioning to the man Sam was speaking with. "He's a good guy. Don't know exactly why he's here, but then, neither does he."

"We ran into our friend at the inn," I said, turning to Cord.

He looked from me to Sam, and she nodded.

"I don't think it's you he hates," she told him.

"Deck, I'd like you to meet Samantha Marquez."

"It's a pleasure, miss."

Sam shot a smirk in Cord's direction, who laughed. "He made the mistake of calling me 'ma'am,'" she explained.

After Ashford introduced the three men he'd brought with him, we went inside, where he got right down to business.

"Here's where we'll start," he said, pointing to a schematic of the main residence. "By the time you go to sleep tonight, the house and barn will be complete, as will the entry gate and most of the perimeter."

I raised a brow, which Decker caught and chuckled. "We don't mess around, Barrett."

"What can I do to help?" I asked.

"Stay out of our way." Deck looked over at Cord. "You in?"

"I am, sir," Cord responded before turning to me. "I helped out at the Roaring Fork when Mr. Ashford and his team put a similar system in place."

"What about lodging?" I asked, realizing I wasn't certain of the state of the bedrooms in the house.

"I, uh, took it upon myself to ask about housekeeping yesterday," said Cord. "Mrs. Miller, who worked for Mrs. Covert for many years, said her staff had cleaned the main residence and the guesthouse per the attorney's request. Not to be morbid or anything, but she mentioned all the bedding was new. I haven't been in this house other than last night, but the guesthouse has five bedrooms."

"This one has eight," said Decker, motioning to the schematic and looking over at Sam. "Me and my guys will stay in the guest quarters if that's all right with you."

"Of course. Stay where you'll be most comfortable."

Decker turned to me. "Cru will get you and Ms. Marquez dialed into the system while the rest of us start installation. Tomorrow, we'll secure any of the perimeter we don't finish tonight, along with the winery and other outbuildings. Cru, you explain how the various checkpoints will work."

"Yes, sir," he responded.

"Deck? A moment?" I asked, motioning for him to follow me to the opposite side of the room.

"I always hate these conversations," he said once we were out of earshot. "You're gonna tell me to send the bill to you, and then I gotta tell you your father already took care of it. I'll save you the trouble of arguing with me since I'm just the messenger. Take it up with your dad and Burns."

Before I could say another word, the man walked out the front door. The rest of the guys, besides Cru, followed him.

"Interesting guy," he said, standing beside me. "Snapper and Kick know him better than I do, but they say he's one of a kind."

I chuckled, then saw Sam from across the room. She had Wanda cradled in her arms. "Give us a minute?"

"You got it. I'll step outside and make a call."

I wrapped both her and the cat in my arms, eliciting a meow out of Wanda loud enough one would think I'd cut off her tail. Sam set her on the floor.

"She doesn't like to be penned in from both sides," she explained.

I looked down at the cat, who was sitting by my feet, swishing her tail like a whip. "See if I'll give you more treats tonight with that kind of behavior."

When Wanda weaved between my legs, Sam giggled. It was a joyous sound.

"I think it's time to check out of the inn. Do you feel comfortable staying here tonight?"

"It sounds like it will be safe enough for royalty, let alone us."

I cupped her cheek, and she kissed me.

"Whatever totally corny thing you were about to say, don't."

I laughed, then went outside and invited Cru back in. "How long will whatever you're showing us take?"

"About twenty minutes for each of you."

"We're going to relocate here tonight. I'd like to get our things from the inn when we're finished."

"You could go now. You'd just be sitting around, waiting, anyway."

"You're sure?"

Cru cocked his head. "Yeah, bro. If I wasn't, I wouldn't have said it." He looked over at Sam. "How long have we all known each other? Twenty years?"

She laughed. "About. Except I'm way younger than the two of you."

He looked at me. "A couple of years younger, right?"

I nodded, and he shook his head.

"You two smartasses are perfect for each other."

I wrapped my arm around Sam and leaned in to kiss her temple. "I'll go to the inn, pack up what we both left there, and return here."

"Won't you need my help?"

I leaned closer and wiggled my eyebrows. "As long as you're okay with me packing your unmentionables, I can handle it on my own."

"You're cute," she said, rolling her eyes.

"I'll admit I've missed seeing you do that."

"Sure, you have," she said, doing it again.

"You'll be all right if I head out? I'll make it quick."

"I'm sure Cru will take care of me." She kissed me and winked.

"Take care but *hands* off." I leveled a glare at him.

I walked out while the two of them were still laughing.

It only took a few minutes to get to the inn, and as I was pulling in, my mobile rang. I picked it up, stunned to see Daphne was calling. I'd forgotten I turned off call blocking once I knew Cru and the others were on their way to East Aurora.

"Hello, Daph. What's up?"

"Beau? Thank God I reached you." She was whispering but sounded as though she'd been crying. "I'm in serious trouble, Beau, and I need help."

"What's going on?"

"Bloody hell. They're back. I have to go. I'll try to ring again as soon as I can."

"Wait—" Before I could ask anything else, I heard the chimes indicating the call had ended.

I packed our bags, gathered the rest of Wanda's things, and called the front desk, requesting assistance. I could manage on my own, but it would take at least three trips to the SUV and back, which would delay my return to Sam. Less than a couple of minutes later, I heard a knock at the door. Given the disgruntled-looking man could still be about, I checked the peephole and saw Grayson.

"Your help is much appreciated," I said after everything was loaded into the back of the vehicle. When I tried to hand him more money, he refused.

"I appreciate it, Mr. Barrett, but you've tipped me more during your stay here than I usually make in three or four months. This one is on me. I'm off in thirty minutes, but if there's anything you need while you're in town, just give me a call. Even if it's bringing you and Ms. Marquez a pizza. My dad owns the best place in town for that, wings, and beef on weck."

"Beef on weck?"

Grayson chuckled. "It's a Western New York thing."

"I'll have to try it sometime."

He handed me the inn's business card. On the back, he'd written his number.

I held it up. "I appreciate this."

"You got it. Oh, and if you need someone to watch Wanda, I'd be happy to do that too."

After thanking him, I pulled away from the Roycroft, feeling a bit sentimental. It was the first place Sam and I had made love. I'd never forget the intimacy or the place where it happened.

I had my mobile on the center console, hoping Daphne would ring me again. My worry for her well-being was increasing by the minute.

Cru offered to help bring the bags into the house after we both insisted Sam remain inside, where it was warm. Once outside, I mentioned the call from Daphne.

"I've no idea where she is, but I fear her choice of words, 'I'm in serious trouble,' means she's in some kind of danger."

Cru frowned and rubbed the back of his neck, something I'd seen him do occasionally when he was particularly stressed.

"Are you all right?" I asked.

"Let's tell Decker what you just told me. Maybe he can help."

Before I could respond, Cru rang him. "We have another situation. Would it be possible for you to return to the main residence?" he asked.

I spun around when I heard Deck say, "I'm right here," after he rounded the corner from the opposite side of the house. "What's up?"

I reiterated the details of Daphne's call.

He held his hand out. "Give me your phone." Cru and I watched him walk over to one of the black SUVs, open the door, and pull out a satchel. "Too damned cold here," he muttered. "Let's go inside."

"Where's Sam?" I asked when we walked through the front door and I didn't see her.

"Settle down, bro. She's probably using the john," said Cru.

"The *john*? Your mother would be appalled at the depth of your impropriety."

Like Sam did so often, Cru rolled his eyes.

"Samantha?" I called out.

"I'm up here," I heard her say from near the stairwell. I took the steps two at a time, carrying both of our bags.

"Exploring?"

Her eyes were wide, and she nodded. "Look at this." She handed me a frame. The photo in it resembled her as a teenager.

"The likeness is almost uncanny."

"That's what I thought. Every picture I've seen of who I'm assuming is Blanche looks like me. Or I guess I look like her. There's got to be a connection; I just can't figure out what in the world it could be."

"Hey, Beau," I heard Cru call out. "We need you back down here."

"What's going on?" Sam asked.

"I'm not certain. When I know more, I'll give you an update."

Based on Sam's scowl, my eye must have twitched.

"I received a call from Daphne. She was whispering, and it sounded as though she'd been crying. After telling me she was in serious trouble and asking for my help, she said she had to ring off and abruptly ended the call."

She studied me, then turned and walked in the opposite direction.

"I'll just be a moment," I shouted down to Cru before following Sam. "What's going on?" I asked when she went into the sitting room I'd discovered the one and only time I was on the second floor. She set the frame on a table.

"Nothing."

"Hold on." I gently grabbed her arm as she tried to walk past me. "Talk to me, Samantha."

"Cru is waiting for you. You should get downstairs."

I shook my head. "He can wait."

Sam folded her arms. "What about Daphne?"

"I'm more concerned about you."

I waited what felt like minutes before she finally spoke.

"Don't lie to me about her."

"It wasn't a lie. I truly don't know more than what I've told you."

"We'll talk about it later."

I felt like a child being scolded. "We'll talk about it now."

Sam raised her brow at my harsh tone. "You know you lied, Beau. Maybe your relationship with Daphne isn't quite as over as you said."

"This is ludicrous. You're angry over a bloody eye twitch?"

Her eyes scrunched. "I'm angry over a *lie*."

"We'll talk about this later." Only after I spoke the words did it dawn on me I'd just repeated the very thing Sam said moments ago.

When she left the room and walked in the opposite direction of the stairs, I didn't follow.

I found Cru and Decker looking at something on the latter's laptop. "What have you discovered?"

"It looks like she's in New York City," said Cru.

"I was able to triangulate her location and set up movement tracking. She's at the Cambria Hotel, and before you say it, the coincidence of her being at a hotel with the same name as the coastal town in California isn't lost on me. You should also know it's a dump."

"I suppose I should go find her." I hoped Sam understood why I had to. However, her reaction of a few minutes ago was out of character. I checked the time, wondering how quickly I could get a flight versus how long it would take to drive from here to there.

"I'll go," said Cru. "You need to stay here."

I was relieved at his offer. "I'm not sure Daph will be comfortable with that." Not that Sam would be if I went. God, this was a conundrum.

I caught a glance between Cru and Decker.

"What?" I demanded.

"Daphne and I…" Cru's voice trailed off.

"Out with it."

"We've gotten closer."

"What in the bloody hell does that mean? You've gotten closer?" Daphne could be in danger, and Cru chose this moment to tell me they were *closer*? The two hardly knew each other.

"Shit, I don't know how to tell you this. We've been…"

"What, dammit? You've been *fucking*?"

"Beau, let Cru be the one to go find her," said Deck, who then motioned with his head behind me.

I looked over my shoulder at Sam, whose expression told me she'd heard every word.

23

Sam

I came downstairs to apologize for overreacting. What I'd just heard told me I hadn't. Beau's response to Cru saying he and Daphne had gotten *closer* justified my fears. Worse than angry, he was jealous.

"Sam, wait," Beau hollered behind me when I raced up the stairs.

What an idiot I'd been to think he moved on from her. That he didn't love her. They had years of history between them. And unlike Beau and me, *all* of theirs were romantic.

I entered the first bedroom I came upon, then closed and locked the door and spun around in a circle, taking it all in. This had to be the master bedroom, given its size, two walk-in closets, and the en suite bath.

Like at the inn, the furniture in the room bore the Roycroft logo. The quilted bedspread was adorned with the same fig-and-vine pattern as was on the blanket in the room Beau and I had shared.

I heard the doorknob jiggle. "Samantha, let me in."

"Go away, Beau. I need a few minutes."

"I've brought Wanda."

The bastard. Of course, he'd think to use my cat to get me to open the door. I momentarily thought about ignoring him, but honestly, I needed her comfort.

"Put her down, then leave."

"You know as well as I do she'll follow me. I'm the provider of sustenance."

He was right. In the last few days, before I could feed her myself, Beau had already done so.

"This ploy only makes you more of an asshole." I unlocked the door and took a step backwards. "I meant what I said. I need a few minutes. Please, don't force me to talk to you right now."

When Beau stalked toward me, I retreated until I felt the bed behind my legs.

"What you heard—"

"Proved you're not over Daphne." I folded my arms and sat down. I shook my head, willing myself not to cry, but the tears came anyway. "I'm such an idiot."

He sat beside me. "You're not an idiot, but you are wrong."

I couldn't look at him. I was too angry.

"What you heard was fear-induced anger. Yes, I was surprised to hear Cru say he and Daphne had been seeing each other. But that isn't what made me angry. It was his hesitancy at a time when every moment counts. That he chose to tell me *now*, when it's probable a woman I've known almost as long as I've known you is in danger, infuriated me." Beau raked his hand through his hair. "I'm getting off subject. The point is, I'm not the person you're accusing me of being, Sam."

"I haven't *accused* you of anything." I took a deep breath. "Look, I get that you're not as over Daphne as you thought you were. It's evident from your reaction as well as your need to lie to me about it."

"You have known me since we were children. Do you truly believe I would profess my undying love for you and also ask you to marry me if I was in love with Daphne?"

"I don't know what to think." I didn't need to see his face to know my words had hurt him. "Traitor," I muttered when Wanda jumped on the bed and stretched out next to him rather than me.

Beau picked her up and set her between us. "Please look at me, Samantha."

When I shook my head, he slid off the bed and knelt in front of me, trapping me between his arms.

"Look into my eyes."

I didn't want to, but that was just being childish. When my gaze met his, I saw the same anguish I was feeling.

"I am not in love with Daphne. I never was in love with her. I know that now. What is between us feels so different. Cutting my own heart out would be easier than walking away from you, not having you in my life, not having you as my wife or the mother of our children. You are everything to me, Samantha. *Everything*."

He moved his hands, which had been resting on the mattress, to my waist.

"You *know* every word I've just said is the truth."

I did, but none of it eased my fear. If Beau changed his mind about us and he and Daphne became a couple again, I would be heartbroken. "Letting you in, opening my heart like I have, has been one of the most difficult things I've ever done. If you—"

"I won't. I swear it."

"You don't know what I was going to say."

Beau's head cocked. "Don't I? How's this? I swear on the memory of my beloved mother I will never walk away from us. More, I will never stop loving you, not only as a friend, but as the woman I was destined to spend my life with."

I dropped my head. "You have no idea how much I want to believe you."

"Then do." Beau put his finger on my chin and raised it so our eyes met again. "I'm sorry for overreacting and sorrier that what you heard made you doubt my love for you." His phone vibrated. "Bloody hell. I must take this."

I tried to move out from between his arms, but he wouldn't budge.

"Daphne? I've got the call on speaker. Sam is here with me."

"Beau, I'm sorry, but I don't know what to do."

It sounded like she was crying. Then we heard jostling, and the call ended.

Beau stood. "We need to—"

"Go!" I followed him as he raced downstairs.

"She just rang again."

Cru was putting a jacket on.

"Hang on," Decker said, holding up a finger in Beau's direction. "There's a private airfield ten miles from here, Cru. Transport will be there before you are. I'm sending the tracker to your phone now so you can see where Daphne is in real time. A team will meet you wherever she's at when you land."

"Copy that," Cru responded. He looked over at Beau.

"Go get her," he said.

Cru nodded and rushed out the door.

"I fear she's in imminent danger," Beau said to Decker, who was watching his screen.

"My team will arrive at her location in under a minute."

When I glanced at Beau, I expected him to be watching the screen too. Instead, his eyes were on me.

When I raised a brow, he took my hand and led me out of the room. "I need to ask you something."

"Go ahead."

"I don't know what Cru or Decker have in mind, but before I make the suggestion, I'm asking how you'd feel if Daphne came here?"

"Beau…"

"I will accept it if you say no. I have practice doing so." He winked. "Unless, of course…"

"I'm not ready to give you an answer."

"Of course. Understood. Perhaps by the time he arrives in the city and they—"

"Not about that. About the other thing."

He smiled and slowly nodded. "Ah, the other thing. As in, whether you'll marry me?"

Rather than answer his direct question, I circled back to the previous one. "If Cru and Daphne are together, how are you going to handle it?"

"Now that the initial shock has worn off, I predict I'll react far better than I did."

"You're sure?"

His eyes bored into mine. "Yes, but it's you who has to make the final decision. This is, after all, your property."

"It isn't yet. Not until the court certifies the trust."

"We've got her!" we heard Decker shout from the other room.

"Tell Cru, or Daphne or whoever, it's okay for them to come here. I mean, if they want to."

Beau nodded, taking my hand and leading me into the room where Decker was on his cell phone.

"That's right, Steel will be waiting with Daphne at the airfield when you land, Cru."

"Offer that he bring her here," said Beau.

Decker held up one finger in Beau's direction, then shook his head.

"Roger that," he said into the phone, then paused. "Good. I'll have the pilot file the flight plan." Decker ended the call. "Cru is taking Daphne to California. It's my understanding he made contact with her parents and they're on their way from Australia."

"Thank God she's safe." Beau breathed a sigh of relief, put his arm around me, and leaned in. "Are we okay?" he whispered.

Were we? I didn't know how to respond. Maybe because I didn't know how *I* was, let alone us. My life had transitioned from a routine—that honestly had turned into a rut—into what felt like a circus.

First, I'd inherited an estate from a woman I didn't know and still had no idea why she'd named me her beneficiary. Then, we ran into someone who, apparently, wasn't happy about it since I could think of no other reason someone would look at me the way he had. Next, I learned Schultz Wineries held a contract that may not be valid to manage the Lilac Lane Winery and the growing operation. And tonight, a bunch of people were installing a high-level security system on the property I still wasn't sure would actually become mine. Before they even got started, Beau had received a call from his ex-girlfriend of many years, saying she was in trouble, and finally, his best friend confessed being "close to her," which Beau had flipped out about. I was beginning to think the rut I'd been in wasn't so bad.

"Sam?"

"We're okay," I murmured. "I'm just really tired."

"I am as well." He motioned to the stairs. "Shall we find a room to lie down in? The one we were in previously seemed quite nice."

"What about Daphne?"

"What do you mean?"

"Do you want to talk to her?"

Beau put his arms around me and rested his forehead against mine like he had so many times in the last few days. "Now that I know she's safe, I have no reason to worry. I trust Cru will sort things out." He took a step back. "We're both exhausted. Let's rest."

"Wait."

"Yes?"

"Are you hungry?"

"Famished, actually. What sounds good?"

I shrugged. "Pizza?"

He pulled a card out of his back pocket. "That sounds fabulous, and I know just the guy to get it for us."

24

Beau

I rang Grayson and ordered enough food for Sam and me, plus plenty to feed Decker and the rest of the guys.

"Would you mind if my sister rides along? She can help get everything out and ready once we arrive," said Grayson.

"Not at all." It occurred to me that Sam might appreciate having another female to chat with.

I went in search of her to give her an update on when the food would be delivered and found her sorting through a storage box.

"What's all that?" I asked.

"Photos mainly, but there are also letters." Sam pointed to a pile on the floor next to her.

"Have you read any?"

She shook her head. "It feels wrong to read Cena's private correspondence."

I lowered myself to the floor and picked one up. "I have several theories. First, if she was concerned about someone reading them, she shouldn't have kept them around. Second, and not to be insensitive, but she's dead, and it seems that everyone else in her family is too. Finally, what if there's something in them that connects the two of you? Wouldn't it be worth reading them to find out?"

"You're right."

"I came to tell you dinner will arrive in approximately thirty minutes."

I peered over her shoulder when Sam didn't appear to have heard me. "Is that Cena and Manley Jr.?" I asked.

She flipped the photo over. "Yes, and it says it was taken in 1974." Sam looked at me more closely. "I wish I had a magnifying glass."

I pulled out my mobile and opened the app that functioned in a similar way.

"Wow. This is cool."

I wouldn't tell her now, but her cell likely had the same feature. "What is it you're trying to get a better look at?"

"Not what. Who."

I looked over her shoulder a second time at a woman standing several feet behind Cena and her son. "Do you recognize her?"

"No. But there's something about her…" She shook her head and returned my mobile.

"What do you say we dive into these tomorrow?" I motioned to the letters. "Unless you'd prefer to do it on your own."

"I'd rather we do it together unless it sounds horribly boring to you."

I held up one of the envelopes. "Are you joking? Solving the great mystery of why a woman seventy-five years your senior, living on the opposite side of the country, left you a veritable fortune? The amateur sleuth in me can't wait to dive in."

Sam both smiled and giggled, warming my heart.

"Have you, by chance, given any further thought to—"

"How about this? When I'm ready to give you an answer, I will."

"You may need reminding."

"That you asked me to marry you? It isn't something I'm going to forget, Beau."

I leaned against the bed and clasped my hands behind my head. "Must mean something to you, then."

Sam set the photo she'd held in her hand down, stood, then put her legs on either side of me and sat, straddling my lap.

I raised a brow. "How long did I say it would be before the food arrives? I'm game if you are."

She put her hands on my shoulders. While doing so might not be considered the sexiest thing she'd ever done, my cock was in disagreement.

"It means *everything*, Beau."

It took me a moment to figure out what she was referring to. "Ah. The proposal."

My darling Samantha rolled her eyes. "No, dinner."

"Hey, get back here," I said, putting my hands on her waist when she attempted to get up.

She shifted forward so the heavenly place between her legs was aligned perfectly with my hardness. If only there weren't so many layers of clothing separating us.

"Do you know how much I love you?" I said, putting my hand on the back of her neck to draw her closer.

"I'm learning."

The kiss I gave her was more powerful, more passionate, and filled with more intensity than any other

I'd given in my life, including to the woman in my arms. The searing desire between us scorched my heart, branding her name there forever.

Sam tensed when an alert sounded on both of our mobiles.

"That was quick," I said when she grabbed hers and showed me the image on the screen. I tapped the talk icon. "Hello, Grayson. Give me a moment to figure out how to open the gate." The instant I said "open," I could see it doing so from the split-image view.

"There's a gate up already?" Sam asked.

"Apparently. As Decker said, they don't mess around. More importantly, dinner has arrived."

I rushed ahead of Sam to help bring the food in; however, by the time I got to the front door, Cord, Snapper, and Kick had most of it in the kitchen already.

"Mr. Barrett, this is my sister, Juniper," said Grayson.

I walked over to shake her outstretched hand. "Both of you, please call me Beau. And this is Samantha," I said when she joined us.

"Sam," she said, shaking the woman's hand like I had.

"Most everyone calls me Juni."

"What a great name," Sam commented.

Juni looked around the kitchen. "I can't remember the last time I was here. It has to have been at least a year. Sorry," she said, waving in front of her face when she teared up. "Miss Cena was such a lovely woman. I miss her."

My eyes met Sam's. "How well did you know her?" I asked.

"Once her eyesight got bad, I'd visit and read to her a few times a week."

"Did she ever talk about her family?"

Juni's eyes met Grayson's, and they both shuddered. "If you mean her nephews, Miss Cena didn't like to think about them, let alone talk about them. Or one of them, anyway. Johnny is okay."

"Who are the others?" I wondered.

"Just one. James, but everyone calls him Jimmy." Juni made a face. "Hard to believe twins could be so different."

"James *Rooker*?" Sam's surprise mirrored my own.

Juni nodded. "That's right."

Out of the corner of my eye, I saw Cord look up at her. Then when he realized I was watching, he looked down again. The name Rooker meant something to him. I was certain of it.

My eyes met Sam's a second time. "Did you say his brother's name is Johnny?"

"That's right. He doesn't live around here, though."

"Where does he live?" Sam asked.

"Colorado."

"We should let you folks eat," said Grayson, nudging his sister.

"It would be great if you could join us for dinner. As you can see, I'm seriously outnumbered," said Sam, motioning to all the men in the room.

"There's nowhere I need to be," Grayson said, looking at Juni.

"Me either, if you're sure you don't mind. I may be biased since our family owns the place, but I love the Goat's food."

Cord looked up. "The Goat?"

"Yeah, have you eaten there?" Juni asked.

Cord shook his head. "There's a bar named the same thing in the town where I'm from."

"Interesting," said Grayson, almost too quietly for anyone to hear. "You said somewhere in Colorado, right?"

Cord nodded since he'd just taken a bite of pizza.

Grayson didn't ask anything else about it, but I was beginning to think there was a *helluva* lot more to this story than anyone was willing to let on. The only connection that hadn't been made, or no one had mentioned yet, was how Sam fit into all of this.

I let her be when she and Juni walked over to the opposite side of the room after they'd loaded their plates with food. Actually, looking at mine versus theirs, mine would fit the description far better.

"Tell me about this place you mentioned in your hometown," I said to Cord, taking the chair beside him.

"The Goat? It's more of a bar than a restaurant. When they're not touring, the band my brother Holt is in plays there sometimes."

"What's the band's name?"

"CB Rice. You ever heard of them?"

My eyes opened wide. "Of course I have. They're brilliant."

"Yeah. They're good."

"Now that you mention it, I remember something about them being from Colorado."

Cord nodded.

I took a drink of the beer Grayson had so kindly included with our order, then leaned forward, keeping my voice low. "I'm sure you're aware, based on the amount of security we're adding if nothing else, that I will do whatever is necessary to protect Samantha. You asked for her consideration in keeping you on here so you would be able to fulfill the terms of your family's trust. However, I will suggest otherwise unless you're prepared to tell me the truth."

Cord shifted so his back was to the other people in the room. "My guess is, like me, you're trying to figure out how Sam fits into all this. I'm doin' the same, except as it relates to me and why the hell I'm here. Until I know who I can trust and who I can't, I'm taking in all the information that presents itself. Eventually, I hope to figure it all out."

"Fair enough. I'd like to suggest that once the security system is in place and everyone else leaves, you, Sam, and I sit down and talk."

"I heard Decker say he figures they'll be done by the end of the day tomorrow."

"Let's tentatively plan to get together for dinner again."

"Okay," Cord mumbled before taking another bite of food.

I looked up at her when Sam approached with Juni on her heels. "What are the two of you up to?"

"I'm going to show Juni the box I found."

"Good idea." I was about to ask if I could join them when Decker walked in the front door. "I'll be up in a bit."

Sam followed my gaze. "Has there been an update about Daphne?"

I shook my head. "Not yet, but I'm about to ask."

"We're just about finished," Decker said when I approached to invite him and the other guys to eat. "Perimeter monitoring is on for the portions we've secured. Either Snapper or Kick can give you the rundown on how it all works."

"Copy that, and please have something to eat," I said, motioning toward the kitchen.

"Boys, dig in," Decker said to the three men who'd followed him inside.

"Any news on Cru and Daphne?"

"Affirmative. They're on their way to Seahorse."

"I see." I wondered if Cru would inform my brother of my whereabouts, given he was on the way to his house. While it didn't matter, I was in no mood for a lecture of any kind from Press.

I followed Decker's gaze to Grayson.

"That's one of the bellmen from the Roycroft. The food you see is from his family's restaurant."

"I know who he is. Where'd Juni go?"

"Upstairs with Sam. How, may I ask, do you know them?"

"It's my business to know every person in the room. Even if they're no longer in it."

Decker walked away, leaving me stunned.

25

"These are amazing," gushed Juni when I showed her the photos I found.

"Some of them aren't labeled," I said, pointing to the pile I'd kept separate.

Instead of looking at any of those, Juni reached over and picked up the one I'd showed Beau earlier. "That one says it's Cena and her son, but the woman in the background wasn't identified. Did Cena have any sisters?"

"No, and whoever it is, is too young to be her brother's wife."

"Maybe she's unrelated."

"Probably. A lot of people have worked at the Lilacs over the years." Juni continued looking through the photos I already had. "Miss Cena really was such a nice woman," she murmured.

"I don't know much about her or her life, but losing a daughter so young must've been devastating. Then having her son die too." I shook my head.

"I don't think she ever got over it. I mean, how could she? Then losing her husband the way she did." Juni's eyes were hooded.

"What happened? If you don't mind me asking."

"He and Miss Cena's brother were killed in a car accident. Manley was only fifty-four when it happened."

"So sad," I said, studying a photo of the husband and wife together when they were younger.

"She never talked much about it, but my grandmother said James was drunk. He was the one driving."

"If James is Cena's brother and he died all those years ago, who has been taking care of the livestock?"

"Her nephew, Jim. He died two weeks before Miss Cena."

"Okay, let me get this straight. Jim recently died, and Jimmy and Johnny are his sons?"

"I know it's confusing. James, Jim, Jimmy, Johnny." Juni rolled her eyes like I did so often, and I laughed.

"You said Jimmy and Johnny are twins?"

"That's right. Jimmy is older by a few minutes. At least that's what Miss Cena said."

"Juni, do you know why Cena left everything to me?"

She shook her head, reached over, and put her hand on mine. "I wish I did. All I can say is there was no way she'd let Jimmy get his hands on it."

"He's that bad?"

"Worse. I think she was afraid he'd blow through all the money as fast as he could and all her and Manley's hard work over the years would be for nothing. I don't know him, but East Aurora isn't a very big place. There are rumors."

"What rumors?"

"You know, that he drinks too much. Which always leads to him being compared to his grandfather—the one Manley was riding with when he died. Somebody said he gambles. Bets on sports a lot too."

"Do you know much about his dad?"

"From everything I've heard, he was a really good guy. Funny how it seems like it skips generations. My family is like that. I mean, not with drinking or anything remotely close to it. My grandmother and I *love* to cook, and my mom—her daughter—hates it. Gran says she doesn't even know how to boil water."

I smiled. "How did Jim die? Do you know?"

"Cancer. From what Miss Cena said, I guess he was sick for a couple of years. Not that you'd know it. I heard he worked up until the day he died." Juni put her hand over her mouth. "Listen to me go on and on. I'm sorry for gossiping so much."

"Please don't apologize. If you hadn't come over tonight, there's a lot I wouldn't know. Actually, there's still a lot I don't know, but at least I know about her nephews. I have one more question if you don't mind."

"I don't mind at all. Just stop me if I start running my mouth again."

"I get that Cena didn't want to leave Jimmy anything, but why didn't she leave it to Johnny?"

"That, I don't know. Like I said, she didn't talk about it much."

"What about Jimmy and Johnny's mom?"

Juni's eyes opened wide, and she reached for the photo we were looking at earlier. "That's who this woman is. Jim's wife, err, their mom." She studied the image. "She had an unusual name. From what I remember when Miss Cena said it, it sounded like a cartoon character. A recent one, though. All I can think of is Cruella and Maleficent, and I know it wasn't one of those."

"Juni, was it Ursula?"

She snapped her finger. "That's it. Wait. Are you okay? You're pale, all of a sudden. Did I say something wrong?"

"How's it going, ladies?" Beau walked into the room, looked at me, then rushed over and sat on the floor next to me. "What's wrong? What's happened?"

I shook my head and rolled my shoulders. "I'm sure it's nothing. Just a coincidence."

"What is?" he pressed, looking from me to Juni.

"Miss Cena's nephew's wife's name was Ursula."

"And?"

Juni shrugged, and they both looked at me.

"My grandmother had a sister named Ursula."

Juni held up the photo. "This is her, but it's kind of hard to see what she looked like."

"Are there any more?" Beau asked.

I shrugged like Juni had.

"Let's look." Beau carefully gathered a stack of photos that he handed to Juni, then handed another to me. "I'll sort through what's left in the box."

"Juni, if you need to leave, it's okay," I told her.

"I'm fine. Gray knows where to find me. Actually, he might not come up here. I'll text him."

I went back through the photos I'd looked at earlier that weren't identified, then divided them into piles whenever a similar-looking person was in the picture. Then I sifted through those Beau had taken out of the box. Most were of Cena with her husband or son, sometimes both. There were also quite a few of Blanche.

"Gray asked if we needed help."

"We could take the lot downstairs," Beau suggested.

"If it's okay, I'd rather not." I motioned to the several piles I had started. "He can come up, though."

"I'll tell him."

When he joined us, Juni showed him the photo of Cena, her son, and the woman she said she thought was Ursula. Beau divided his set, and Grayson began sorting half of it.

They both added photos to the piles I'd already started at a far quicker pace than I was.

"Sorry, I'm taking so much longer than you all are," I said, looking at them, then Beau.

He leaned over and kissed me. "Take all the time you need, my love. Something tells me you're holding your ancestry in your hands."

While Ursula was my grandmother's sister's name, and even if by some crazy coincidence it was her, it still didn't explain why Cena would leave her entire estate to her niece-in-law's grandniece.

After an hour, I'd yawned several times in quick succession and it was getting harder to focus on the photos.

"What do you say we call it a night?" said Beau when I leaned into him and rested my head on his shoulder.

"Do you want us to clean all this up?" Juni asked.

"Thanks, but no. I'll keep working on it tomorrow."

As if on cue, Wanda jumped off the bed where she'd been perched for the last couple of hours and headed straight for the piles of pictures.

"Not so fast," said Beau, scooping her into his arms.

"We could put them in one of the other bedrooms and close the door," Juni suggested.

Before I could start gathering any, Beau handed Wanda to me. "You tend to your cat-daughter, and we'll handle this."

I burst out laughing. "Cat-daughter?"

He shrugged. "What else would you call her?"

"Fur baby?"

He leaned over and kissed my forehead. "Clever, but the added eye roll is what really nailed it."

"I didn't make that up. It's what everyone says."

"Grayson, do you refer to your cat as your fur baby?" Beau asked.

"Never."

"Juni?"

"Um, no, but—"

Beau held up his hand. "I think we've effectively established it's not what *everyone* says."

I couldn't just watch them clean up my mess without feeling guilty, so I carried Wanda into the bathroom with me and shut the door.

"I wish Cena was here to explain all this. I guess if she were still here, I wouldn't be. You'd think she would've left me a letter or something, though. Wouldn't you?"

Wanda did look up at me briefly, then shut her eyes and purred.

"And if there was a letter, you'd think the lawyer would've included it in what he sent to me, right?"

"Right," said Beau, opening the door. "Everything's put away. Safe for you and Wanda to come out now."

"Beau? Maybe we should ask the lawyer to check again for a letter."

He nodded. "That reminds me. He'll be here at nine tomorrow morning. I asked if he could come a bit later, but he said he has another meeting at ten."

"Nine's fine."

Beau raised a brow.

"What? I've been known to get up that early."

"Nine here is six in California."

"I appreciate you pointing that out. Now, I'll never get to sleep nor will I want to get up at nine tomorrow."

"I'll see what creative way to wake you I can come up with." He winked.

I brushed my teeth and was getting ready to crawl into bed when a thought occurred to me. "Wait. Do you think it's weird to sleep in here?"

"Cord said the housekeeper mentioned all the bedding was new. Is that your concern, or is there something else?"

"I'm sleeping in a bed in a room that belonged to a person I don't even know."

Beau lay down and pulled back the sheets. "It's no different than staying in a hotel room. We don't know who slept there last, either."

I shuddered. "Great. Now, I'll never feel comfortable at a hotel again."

"Samantha, if you'd prefer not to stay here tonight, we can find other accommodations."

"We can't go back to the Roycroft now that I know strangers slept there before me too."

He rolled his eyes. "Get in bed, my love."

Unable to get the idea that I was sleeping in a stranger's room out of my head, I worried I'd toss and turn. Instead, I think I conked out shortly after my head hit the pillow.

I felt certain Beau's creative way of waking me up would be sexual, but he surprised me with breakfast in bed instead. He set the tray down on a table by the window. "Good morning, my darling." He ruffled Wanda's fur. "And you too, Sam."

I stuck my tongue out at him and stretched my arms over my head, remembering then that I was naked when the sheet slipped down. I yanked it back up when Beau wriggled his eyebrows. "How long have you been awake?" I asked.

He went into the bathroom and came out with a plush terry-cloth robe.

"Where did this come from? I don't remember seeing this last night."

"Did you think I only brought gifts for our *fur baby*?"

He wrapped it around me when I got out of bed.

"I should feed Wanda." I looked at the bed but didn't see her. "Where is she?"

Beau pointed to a rug near another window. "Already fed and taking her morning nap."

I padded over to the table and sat when he pulled a chair out for me. "This is very sweet of you."

"I'll remind you that, if you give me the answer I desire, this could be the way you start every morning."

"If I said I'd marry you, you'll commit to bringing me breakfast in bed every morning? After feeding Wanda first, of course."

He leaned down and kissed my forehead. "At the very least, I will commit to serving you breakfast on a table. Will that do?" He poured each of us coffee, then sat in the chair opposite mine.

"So beautiful," I said, pointing to the view of the snow-covered grounds.

"Mmm. Very beautiful." Beau scooted his chair closer and nuzzled my neck. "I wish we had time for more of this, but the attorney will be here in twenty minutes."

"*Twenty minutes?* I still need to shower." I pushed the chair back.

"Sam, sit down and finish your breakfast. If you are not ready when he gets here, I will keep him entertained with witty banter and small talk."

"I thought he had a meeting at ten."

"Right. Ten minutes tops of small talk only. No time for witty banter."

"It's even warm," I mewled, picking up one of the two chocolate croissants. "Did you go to a bakery this morning?"

"Once again, Grayson came to my rescue. I'm thinking of hiring him as my personal assistant. What? Why did that garner an eye roll? I'm serious."

"*Your* personal assistant? I doubt he'd be interested."

"Well, he's certainly not going to be yours. Juni, on the other hand, could be."

"That's sexist."

"No, my love. That's possessive."

I made it downstairs with a few minutes to spare and found Beau in the kitchen with Decker.

"I was about to give Beau my report on some of the characters associated with the Lilacs. You should sit in on it too."

"I asked Cru to do some checking on Cord, Hoss Schultz, and also James Rooker," Beau explained.

"Depending on which one you're talking about, I can tell you about James Rooker," I said.

Decker shut his laptop. "Go ahead."

"I hope I get this right. James Rooker was Cena's brother. According to what Juni told me, he was driving drunk and had an accident. Manley, that's Cena's husband, was in the car with him. Both men died."

Beau looked over at Decker, who nodded.

"Jim Rooker is James' son. Apparently, he was a good guy. He recently passed away from cancer only a couple of weeks before Cena did. Juni said he worked until the day he died."

"Got it," said Decker.

"Then there's Jimmy and Johnny. They're Jim's sons. They're twins, and Jimmy's older. Anyway, Johnny lives in Colorado." I looked up at Decker. "I guess you already know that part."

"I know all of it, but continue anyway."

"Juni said Cena didn't want to leave anything to Jimmy because she was afraid he'd blow right through it all." I folded my hands on my lap. "That's all I know. Oh, I asked why Cena didn't leave it all to Johnny, and she said she didn't know. She also has no idea how I got involved."

"That it?" Decker asked.

"I think so."

"Now, I'll tell you what I know." He reopened his laptop and turned to Beau. "We'll start with Cord. He's on the up-and-up, by the way. His mother, Patricia, was Cena's niece. She was only ten when her father died—let's continue referring to him as James. Her brother, Jim, was quite a bit older than her, and the two were never close. I haven't pieced it all together yet, but somehow, she ended up in Colorado."

All three of our phones chimed simultaneously.

"The attorney has arrived," said Beau.

"Let him in, but tell him to cool his jets for a few."

Beau stood and walked a few feet away.

"Back to Patricia. Cord said neither he nor any of his siblings knew anything about his mother's family. That's part of what I haven't pieced together yet."

"Did he tell you why he was here?"

Decker nodded. "The trust. I know Cord's older brother, and he went through the same shit. I tried findin' more about it then and got nowhere. Anyway, one thing I was able to find out is that Cena did leave something to Johnny. Actually, he got his inheritance early with the stipulation that Jimmy never find out about it. That was no skin off John's back, considerin' he has the same opinion of his brother everyone else seems to have."

I wanted to ask what Cena left him, but it was none of my business. Actually, it felt like everything I'd learned since the day I received the packet from the lawyer was none of my business.

"John's got a ranch in Black Forest, Colorado. Bigger than this place, in fact. That was Cena's doin'. I don't know how well you know Colorado, but Crested Butte, where Patricia settled, is about five hours from where John is, so no connection there, it seems."

"The lawyer is insisting he needs to talk to us immediately," said Beau.

"For Christ's sake," Decker muttered. "You'd think he'd want to get more billable hours in, sittin' and waitin'."

"Okay to let him in?"

Decker nodded. "I'll be in the other room, but don't worry, I'll be listenin'."

"Miss Marquez," Mr. Creola said as he rushed in the front door after Beau opened it. "I received a notification from the court early this morning. Mrs. Covert's will and trust are being contested."

"Let me guess. By James Rooker?" said Decker, who'd apparently decided *not* to wait in the other room.

"Who are you?" the attorney asked.

"Decker Ashford, and continue with what you were saying, Paul."

The man's eyes scrunched, and he cleared his throat. "As I said, James Rooker has filed for an immediate injunction to stop you from taking possession of the Lilacs."

"On what grounds?" Beau asked.

Mr. Creola set an envelope on the table and removed his coat.

"I'll take that for you," I offered, returning to where they all stood after I draped it over a chair.

"As far as grounds, he's citing a previous trust's stipulation that the Lilacs, along with the rest of the estate, can only be left to a direct descendant."

"Whose descendant? Cena's or Manley's?" Decker asked.

The lawyer glared at him. "I don't know, but I've requested the attorney representing Mr. Rooker produce it immediately as part of discovery."

"Lemme guess. If there are no direct descendants, the estate is to be liquidated and given to a named charity," said Decker.

"Again, I do not have the document as of yet, sir."

"Bet ya a million bucks," Decker said under his breath.

"I thought trusts were used because they couldn't be challenged."

Mr. Creola looked over at me and sighed. "I'm sorry to say something like this is an exception."

"Does this mean I have to leave?" I asked.

"Not yet. He's only filed for the injunction. It hasn't been granted yet. As soon as I receive the documents I've requested, I'll be in touch. I expect them later today."

Mr. Creola stood and looked around for his coat.

"Samantha," murmured Beau. "Was there something else you wanted to ask about?"

"Right. This might not matter anymore, but I wanted to be sure Mrs. Covert hadn't left a letter for me."

The attorney blinked a couple of times. "If she had, it would've been included in what was delivered to you."

"That's what I figured."

"What about a safe-deposit box?" Decker asked.

"I was about to suggest the same thing," said Beau.

"Yes, there is one. However, until the injunction request is denied, the court cannot certify the trust. Meaning, nothing is actually yours until that happens."

Beau walked Mr. Creola to the door.

"You okay?" Decker asked.

"I always knew it wasn't real." That didn't change my disappointment, though. Not because of the money or even the estate. Last night, Beau had said he felt as though I was holding my ancestry in my hands. The more I looked through the photos, the more I'd started to believe it too.

"Okay, y'all ready for the rest I have to tell you?" Decker asked when Beau returned to where we waited.

26

Beau

Sam's disappointment was etched on her face. I was far more worried about her than I was about anything else Decker had to tell us.

"First, let's talk about the injunction request. Regardless of whether the other trust stipulates the beneficiary be the direct descendant of Manley or Cena, it's irrelevant as far as James Rooker is concerned, since he is neither." Decker chuckled, "I'd say he isn't smart enough to know the definition, but he didn't file with the court; an attorney did. On the other hand, I've known plenty of lawyers who didn't know their hind end from a hole in the wall."

"What would his motive be for filing, then?" I asked.

"I'm not sure, unless he's got somethin' up his sleeve in regard to a delay in the trust being certified."

"Look, it's obvious the Rookers are related to Cena. I'm not. So, in all fairness, shouldn't they be the ones to inherit? I mean, it wouldn't all go to Jimmy and

Johnny Rooker. Some of it would go to Cord and his siblings, right?"

Decker stroked his beard. "They may be required to prove their mother was Cena's niece, but that would be easy enough to do. A simple DNA test would confirm it." His eyes were scrunched as he looked off into the distance. "What about you? Have you ever gotten one of those tests?"

"I haven't," Sam responded.

"Let's get that in the works. The results take a bit to come back, but I can pull some strings to make it happen quicker."

"What good would that do?" she asked.

"If anyone from Cena's family took one, there'd be a connection established," I explained.

"If we make the request," Decker qualified. "Which is possible to do privately when law enforcement is involved." He winked.

"What do I have to do?" Sam asked.

"I'll take care of getting it started. Easiest is a mouth swab."

Decker rested against his chair and rubbed his hands together. "Let's talk about Hoss Schultz. As you've probably guessed, the guy has questionable business tactics. Besides Cord reporting he saw Rooker talking with him, there's no connection between the two men that I've been able to find. Yet anyway."

"James, err, Jimmy Rooker is the man we saw at the pub?" I asked.

"Affirmative." Decker turned his laptop so Sam and I could see the screen. On it were several surveillance photos of him, including those taken that night as well as at the Roycroft. "He hasn't set foot on the premises in the hours since we've activated security. However, if he does at anytime in the future. We'll know it."

"Beau and I met with the son of the attorney who drew up the contract between Lilac Lane Winery and Schultz Wineries. He suggested we question the validity of the contract, but I guess, for now, I really can't." Sam looked over at me. "I don't know what to do, Beau. Should we just return to California now?"

Before I could answer, Decker did. "I know this is difficult to fathom, but I feel certain you have a DNA connection to Mrs. Covert. I do not believe she would have left all this to you if there wasn't one."

She shook her head. "You're right about me not fathoming it."

"Samantha, there is still the matter of Ursula Rooker and whether she was your grandmother's sister." I turned to Decker. "We have yet to find a second photo of the woman. Juni believes she may be in the background of one with Cena and Manley Jr."

"Interesting," he said under his breath. "Back to Hoss Schultz. My recommendation is that you eventually terminate the contract with Schultz Wineries. In the meantime, Snapper and Kick will be meeting with him this afternoon, posing as investors in another New York State winery interested in having Schultz manage the growing operation and the winery. That meeting will be off-site, so if the two of you have an interest in checking out the Lilac Lane facilities, it would be a good time to do it."

"I'm not sure it's a good idea for me to get further invested in this place."

I understood her hesitation. "As Decker said, it seems logical to think Cena was aware of the previous trust and its stipulations. Conversely, it is illogical to think she'd put forth the effort to make you her beneficiary if there wasn't some kind of connection."

My eyes met Decker's when Sam looked away. I had no doubt she was overwhelmed and emotional.

"If you'll both excuse me, I have a couple of calls to make." Decker stood and went outside.

"Hey," I said, putting my hand on Sam's back.

She turned to me, and as I'd expected, she was crying.

"I never should've come here. Please understand I appreciate everything you've done, but my gut was telling me there was no way this could be real. I should've listened."

I drew her into my arms. "Giving up now is premature, my love."

Sam shook her head. "I can't do this. It has nothing to do with the money or the property or the house. Although I do love it. It's more that, for a very short amount of time, I believed—" She broke down, burying her face in my chest.

"Shh," I soothed, stroking her hair. "What did you believe?"

"That I wasn't...alone anymore."

I pulled back and put my finger on her chin. When she looked up at me, I kissed away the tears on her cheeks. "You are not alone. You have me."

"You know what I mean. I've never had a family, Beau."

"*We* are a family, and we have a fur baby to prove it." She smiled.

"Someday, I hope we'll add more. Perhaps even from the Homo sapiens species."

"It would be nice to think Cena and I were related. Equally as sad as finding out we're not is that I never got to know her."

"The way I see it, that is the biggest tragedy of all."

"She knew who I was for over a year. Why didn't she reach out?"

"Given her age, along with Juni saying her eyesight was failing, maybe she didn't have the ability to do so."

Sam sighed. "You're right."

"Yes, I often am, not that you're usually so quick to agree."

Sam smiled again, leaned up, and kissed me. "I love you, Beau."

"And I love you, my darling." I looked at the time. It was nearing eleven. "What do you say we wrap up with Decker, have lunch, then recommence looking through photos?"

"I also want to call the church today and see what the secretary can tell me about the Covert family."

"That's the spirit. We'll continue moving forward until such time when we deem we shouldn't. Which, I predict, will not happen." I leaned back and rubbed my stomach. "Any requests for lunch?"

Sam stood and walked to the refrigerator. "Leftover pizza?"

"Sounds perfect."

Her eyes were wide. "Hot or cold?"

My eyes scrunched. "Cold, of course. Who would want it hot?"

"Me. Probably anyone who has ever eaten leftover pizza."

"Clearly, I've eaten it. Are you suggesting otherwise?"

This time, she raised a brow.

"What?" I demanded. "You *know* I'm not lying."

"I'm just surprised you eat leftovers at all when you could have food delivered anytime you want it."

"I see." I stood and joined her in front of the open refrigerator. "You're roundaboutly saying I only consume that which is freshly prepared?"

"No, but…"

"I'd like to suggest you consider that, in this instance, it's you who's being the snob, Samantha."

She opened her mouth to speak, then shut it.

"No pithy comeback?"

"You did have Grayson deliver food to you twice in the last few hours."

I put my arms around her waist. "You make a good point. However, most of what I ordered was for you. Well, and for others."

She pulled the box from a shelf and held it open. When I reached in, she snapped it closed on my hand, then we both laughed uproariously.

"I do love you so," I said when we stopped.

She scooted under my arm, retrieved a plate from the cupboard, then froze without placing it on the counter.

"What?" I asked, rushing over to her. I followed her line of sight to the photo taped on the inside of the door. "Who is that?" I asked.

Sam gently pulled it off and turned it over. When her knees gave out, I wrapped my arm around her waist and held her upright.

"What is it?" I asked.

She handed me the photo. On the back was written, "Manley Jr. and Pilar, 1974." The couple were in a driveway that looked much like that of the Lilacs, and they were holding hands.

I led Sam over to the table and pulled out a chair for her before turning it and the one beside it so we were facing each other when I took a seat.

"Talk to me," I whispered.

"My mother was born in 1975."

27

Sam

Beau put his hands on my shoulders. "This is fantastic news, Samantha. Bit of shock, but wonderful, nonetheless."

I stared into his eyes. Was it? "Does it prove anything beyond my grandmother and Cena's son knew each other?"

The front door opened, and Decker stuck his head inside. "Should I come back later?"

Beau turned to me. "I think we should tell him."

I nodded.

Decker walked over and sat on the opposite side of the table. "What do you want to tell me?"

I handed him the photo. "I found this taped inside the cupboard door."

He looked at both sides. "Pilar is your grandmother."

"Yes," I responded, even though he hadn't phrased it as a question. "I'm not sure what a single photo proves, though."

"When was your mother born?" he asked.

"The year after what's shown on the photo."

"That's what I thought."

"Again, what does it prove? That Cena suspected my grandmother had a baby?"

"What about the photos of you?" Beau reminded me.

"What photos?" Decker asked.

"Let me see if I can find them." Beau didn't move until I nodded. "I think they're just in the other room."

"Weird place to put a photo," I muttered, fingering the one Decker handed back to me.

"Not really. There were pictures taped inside cupboards in the house where I lived as a teenager. I think people did that back in the day, especially when it was a place they looked often. Quick reminder of someone they cared about."

"Here they are," said Beau, handing the envelope to Decker.

He removed each of the photos and set them side by side on the table, then raised his head and glared at Beau.

"What?"

"You just remembered these now?"

"My apologies," he responded under his breath when Decker pulled out his cell phone. Beau glanced at me, and I shrugged. I hadn't thought about them, either.

"Hey, I need you up at the main residence as soon as you can get here." He ended the call and set his phone on the table. "Anything else you've neglected to tell me about?"

"I'm sorry, I didn't think—"

Decker held up his hand. "Not you, Sam. Him." When he winked, I let out the breath I was holding. Apparently, Beau hadn't seen it, given his scowl.

"He's joking," I whispered.

"Hang on." Decker picked up his phone again and typed something on the screen, then set it down in the same place. "I asked Cord to meet us here too. If he has had his DNA run, that's the quickest way to prove you're related to Cena. If he hasn't, we'll submit his test at the same time as yours."

"I hadn't thought about that. If I am related to Cena, it would mean Cord and I are cousins." Something about thinking we might be made me really happy. "I hope I'm not setting myself up for more disappoint-ment," I added under my breath.

"Remember, we're going to continue moving forward," said Beau, leaning close and kissing my cheek.

Our eyes met, and neither of us looked away. What would've happened if I hadn't called and asked for his help? What if I'd just tossed the envelope in the trash, believing it was a hoax? Would either Beau or I ever have had the guts to admit our feelings? Would we even have realized them?

That we loved each other was so much bigger, so much more important than this house, the estate, the money, even finding out I had a family I never realized I had.

If it all disappeared in the next hour, the most important person in my life would still be right beside me. As he'd said, we were a family. Beau and me. And Wanda. That alone proved how much he loved me. I'd never admit it to him, but he took better care of my cat than I did.

"How I wish I knew what you were thinking," he murmured.

I leaned forward and kissed his neck right beneath his ear. "Yes," I whispered.

He pulled back and looked at me with scrunched eyes. "Yes?"

I smiled. "Yes."

He smiled too. "Yes?" Each time he said it, his voice got louder.

My eyes filled with tears, and I nodded.

Beau stood and pulled me up with him, gathering me in his arms and spinning us both in a circle. "She said yes!"

Out of the corner of my eye, I saw Decker watching the two of us. His smile was as broad as Beau's and mine.

"I'll get it," he said when someone knocked on the door, probably because Beau still held me in his arms and we were kissing.

"We celebrating something?" Cord asked. "Did you figure out how you're connected to Mrs. Covert?"

"Nah, I think they're gettin' married," I heard Decker tell him.

Beau set me on my feet. "Yes, we're getting married, but we also believe we found a link between Cena and Sam." He picked up the photo and handed it to Cord. "Pilar is Sam's grandmother."

Cord's eyes opened wide.

"That alone doesn't prove anything in terms of Sam being related to Cena. It'll take DNA to make that determination. That's where you come in. Have you ever had yours tested?" Decker asked.

"I haven't, sir."

"In that case, both you and Sam will get tested at the same time. There's a version of the test law enforcement can push to be expedited. It only takes an hour or two to get the results, depending on how busy the lab is. It'll be definitive enough."

"Sure. Of course."

"There's a place in town that has the kits. They said they can get it to the lab right away. While you do that, I'll check on my guys' progress."

Decker gave Beau the address of the drugstore.

"Perhaps, while we're out, we could get something freshly prepared for lunch," said Beau, winking at me once we were in the SUV. "Cord, do you have time to join us?"

"Sure. I mean, you're engaged, right? And Sam might be my cousin. I'd say we should celebrate."

I looked over the seat at him and smiled. "I hope we are, Cord."

"Me too."

As Decker said, the DNA test was simple and only took a couple of minutes for each of us. Beau spent the time researching where to have lunch.

"I'll forewarn you that by the time we order and our food is served, Beau will know everyone in the place," I told Cord as we walked out of the drugstore.

I glanced at him over my shoulder when he didn't respond. His eyes were hooded. Beau had a similar expression. I followed their line of sight. "I don't see anything."

"Jimmy Rooker," Beau muttered.

"There's a place we could eat in the next town over. It's more populated than East Aurora, and if we see him there, we'll know he's tailing us," Cord suggested.

Once we were in the vehicle, Beau said he'd call Decker.

"He's asked you text him the name and address of where we're going. He'll have two of his guys there, waiting," he said to Cord after ending the brief call.

I'd ask if this level of caution was necessary, but given what the estate was worth, who knew what Jimmy was desperate enough to do to get his hands on it?

"Where's the wedding?" Cord asked.

"We haven't discussed it," said Beau, looking over at me. "She only said yes an hour ago. I don't want to push her."

I laughed. "Probably in Napa since that's where Beau's father and brother are."

"Or Cambria, since we have many friends there."

"I'm guessing both are in California," said Cord.

"That's right," Beau told him.

Neither place thrilled me that much. Maybe once Beau and I had a chance to talk about it enough to set a date, I'd warm up to one or both.

"We could always do it here."

I looked over at Beau to see if he was joking. It didn't appear he was. I wouldn't put him on the spot in front of Cord, but when we were alone later, I'd ask if he'd consider it. Not having the ceremony close to home would matter more to him than me since he had more friends and family there than I did.

"Have you heard from Cru?" I asked.

He looked out the driver's side window and shook his head. It was something else I should've waited until we were alone to ask.

"Here's the place. I hope you don't mind having roast beef again," said Cord. "They have other stuff, though, if you do mind." Beau pulled into the parking lot of a place that looked as though it had once been a house, like the restaurant we ate at the first night when we met Mr. Allen and his son.

"It says it's been here since 1837," I said, pointing to the sign when Beau opened my door.

"Must be quite good, then."

Walking in felt like we'd stepped back in time. The waitresses all wore pristine white uniforms with green aprons, and the men behind the bar wore white shirts and bow ties.

Black-and-white photos lined the walls throughout the place, and when the waitress took our order, I asked if it would be okay for me to walk around to look at them.

"That's what they're here for, honey," she said, winking.

The three of us stood, and because the space was tight, Cord went in one direction and Beau and I went in the other. Many of the images were of customers throughout the years.

"Hey, look at this," Cord said from the other side of the room.

"Is that Cena and Manley?" Beau asked.

I took a closer look. "It is, and it says it was taken in 1975, the same year Manley died." The two were holding hands, sitting close enough that their arms touched. "They look so in love," I murmured.

"And they were," said an older gentleman sitting at an adjacent table.

"Did you know them?" I asked.

"Very well. Their son and I went to school together, so I was frequently invited to the Lilacs. Are you familiar with the place?"

"We are," Beau responded. "Quite lovely."

The man rested his hand on his chin. "They used to have amazing parties there in those days. Any occasion they could think of. Hell of a thing, the way Manley died. Worse was how his son went."

"What do you mean?" I asked.

"Both were killed in car accidents, several years apart, of course. With Junior, though, rumor was his brakes had been tampered with. Couldn't ever prove it. The car veered off the road and went over an embankment straight into Buffalo Creek. The condition of the car made it nearly impossible to prove anything."

"Wow," I said under my breath.

The man shook his head. "Some say it was his good-for-nothing nephew who did the tampering. Others say Junior had been drinking, but I knew better. After losing his dad that way, he never would've drove while intoxicated."

I looked beyond the man to our table, where the waitress had delivered our food. Beau noticed the same thing.

"Thank you for your time," he said, reaching out to shake the man's hand.

"You look a lot like the pictures of Blanche they had in practically every room at the Lilacs. That was Junior's sister. He was only four when she died. You some relation?"

"Distant," I murmured.

"Enjoy your lunch," he said, raising his hand in a wave.

"Wow," Cord said under his breath once we'd taken our seats. "Someone should write a book about the Coverts."

I agreed.

"No sign of Rooker," said Beau, glancing at his phone after we'd finished eating. "Decker reminded us that the winery will be empty this afternoon if we want to take a look at it."

"Can I come along?" Cord asked. "I've never been in the place."

Since it was a nice day and most of the snow had melted, Beau parked near the main house, and the three of us walked to the winery.

Growing up in the Central Coast of California's wine region, I'd been in several. More, after I went to work for Stave. The Lilac Lane building was impressive, given the relatively low number of hectares dedicated to vineyards as well as the estimated number of cases they released each year.

For fermentation, there were ample stainless steel tanks, plus barrel rooms. Their harvest production area was equally impressive.

"Thoughts?" Beau said, grinning when I came back from taking a look at the tasting room.

"Someone sunk a lot of money into this place. They could easily produce three or four times the amount of wine they've averaged. They'd need more fruit, but my guess is that wouldn't be hard to come by."

Cord looked from Beau to me and back again.

"I have a degree in ag business. My emphasis was in growing and grafting Vitis vinifera." When I saw his eyes glaze over, I stopped talking and laughed. "Sorry. I'd probably have the same look on my face if you tried to talk to me about cows."

Cord chuckled too. "Cattle."

"I want to inspect the tanks, air and water lines, as well as take a look at their bottling area," said Beau.

"Can I help?" Cord asked.

"Yes, but don't be surprised if you smell a bit like vinegar when we're finished."

I was about to follow them into the other room when two alerts went off on my phone. The first was a reminder for me to call the church secretary. The second was a text from Juni, saying she had more information about Cena's family and was wondering if she could stop by.

By the time I got to the fermentation area, Beau was lying on the concrete floor, inspecting the area beneath one of the tanks.

"Hey, I'm going to head up to the house. I have a call to make to the church, and Juni wants to stop by."

"Right. I can pick up where I left off tomorrow."

"Go ahead and finish your inspection now. Hoss might be back tomorrow."

"Will you be all right, walking up to the house alone?"

Beau couldn't see him, but Cord's eyes opened wide.

"Yes, future husband, I can manage a ten-minute walk on my own."

He scooted out from under the tank and looked at Cord. "She loves me."

He laughed. "That, she does. If you want, though, I can walk with her."

I rolled my eyes. "First of all, don't talk about me like I'm not standing here. Second, isn't the fancy-schmancy security system supposed to keep me safe?"

"Affirmative," said Beau, sliding beneath a second tank. "In fact, I received word from Decker a few minutes ago, saying installation as well as testing was complete."

"Then, I'll see you later."

"Wait." Beau slid out again, got to his feet, and approached me.

I waved a hand in front of my face. "You're going to need winery clothes. Those already smell."

"Yeah?" He stepped forward, acting like he was going to rub fermented residue all over me.

I giggled and raced toward the door.

"I love you," I hollered after me.

"Love you too," said Cord, winking.

"Hey," Beau snapped at him.

He held up both of his hands. "Like a cousin, man. Chill out."

Beau blew me a kiss, and I walked out into the sunshine. I surveyed the property as I went, incredulous that a place this beautiful might really be mine. As much as I tried to steel myself against getting my hopes up, I couldn't help it. Add in that Cord seemed as happy as I was about learning we might be cousins, and it made it even better.

When I was younger, I'd dreamed of having a big family, which was kind of ridiculous since it was just my mom and me. Then, just me. Given the few relationships I was in hadn't lasted very long, I didn't hold out much hope for having kids either.

It felt like a dream when Beau said, "I want to marry you and fill that big house that's about to become yours with as many children as I can convince you to bear."

I looked at it in the distance, imagining how great it would be to raise children in it. It was almost too perfect, not that I'd let those kinds of thoughts ruin my day.

Beau and I were getting married. It would take a bit for me to get used to the fact we were. I could count on him to remind me, though. Probably at least once an hour.

I loved him *so* much. It was like once I allowed myself to admit it, the floodgates had opened and my entire body was filled with love for Beau.

When I stumbled on a rock, I realized I should be paying attention to the ground in front of me instead of letting my mind drift. Still, even after stubbing my toe, I felt better, happier, more content than I ever remembered in my life. If I didn't think I'd trip and break my neck, I'd skip the rest of the way to the house.

For a split second, I thought the arm that snaked around my waist was Beau's. But he didn't smell like well whiskey. When the man covered my mouth with his hand and stuck a gun in my side, I had a feeling I knew exactly who it was—*Jimmy Rooker*.

"Keep walking," he said, jamming the gun harder into my side. "That's it. Just stay nice and calm, and this will all be over before you know it." His hand moved slightly, and I opened my mouth, biting down as hard as I could.

He cried out, "*You fucking bitch!*" but didn't let me go or stop walking. He did move his hand away from my mouth.

At the same time, the phone I had in my pocket went off with the sound of an alarm.

"What the fuck was that?"

"Reminder," I blurted, hoping it would stop. It did.

"You scream, and this gun goes off here and now. You're nothin'. Just a blip on the radar of somethin' I've been waitin' on my whole life. Once I get rid of you, everything you see will belong to me. The way it should've been all along."

"It was you who tampered with Manley's car, wasn't it?" Thinking about what the man in the restaurant had said.

"Damn ol' asshole. Spent his whole life trying to find the slut he got pregnant." He laughed. "And then, when he finally does…BAM…he's already dead, and so is the piece of shit offspring they had. That was one of the best days of my life, I'll tell ya." He pressed the gun harder. "Then you come along just when I thought everything was tied up in a nice little bow. All that was left was gettin' rid of *Junior*. I had no idea he'd tell his bitch of a mama. I should've, though. Fuckin' Mama's boy. Since she was the one who ran the slut off, who knew she'd want anything to do with the likes of you?"

All at once, Rooker froze. I stumbled at his abrupt stop, but he kept his arm around my waist.

"Keep your head down, Sam!" I heard Decker shout. "Let her go, Rooker. Take a look around you. If you don't, ten bullets are gonna hit your worthless piece-of-shit brain simultaneously. You've got to the count of three. One, two—"

Jimmy pushed me away from him, and I fell to the ground. When I looked up, Beau was racing toward me. He got between Rooker and me, picked me up, and ran. I heard one shot fired as he carried me into the woods, and nothing after that.

When he got to the bank of the pond, he set me on a bench near the edge and fell to his knees in front of me.

"My God," he moaned, wrapping his arms around me. I could feel the dampness from his tears. "Samantha, my love. I almost lost you." He repeated those words over and over again while we both held each other and cried.

"Beau? Sam?" I heard Cord calling our names. Beau eased away from me, and I moved his hair from his forehead. His pupils were dilated, and his expression anguished.

"I'm okay. I'm fine," I said. "Come back to me, Beau."

"I've never been so afraid of anything in my life," he said right before I brought my lips to his.

"Not even teaching me to drive?"

He smiled, at least, and immediately kissed me again, our mouths devouring as our hands traveled the length of each other's bodies, as if touching each other proved we were both okay.

"There you guys are," I heard Cord again, now he sounded a few feet from us. "Decker told me to give you the all clear. Cops just got here. Jimmy's, uh, immobilized, but his wound isn't life-threatening."

"He's alive?" I asked, looking over at Cord.

"Yeah."

"I heard a gunshot."

"About that…"

"*What* about it?" asked Beau, finally turning to look at him.

"Decker's really pissed at me. I shot the fucker's kneecap out."

Both Beau and I stared at him.

"What? I couldn't let him get away with almost killing my cousin. I had to make him pay somehow."

By then, Cord was close enough that I could reach out and touch his arm. I would've hugged him, but Beau refused to let me go.

28

Beau

If she would've let me, I would have carried Samantha from the pond to the house. As it was, as much of me had to be touching as much of her as possible. One arm was around her, and with the opposite hand, I gripped hers.

It was my fault that fucking *sonuvabitch* got his hands on her. I never should've let her walk to the house alone, and I would never, ever let her out of my sight again.

I'd almost lost the most precious, the most beloved person in my life, and if I had, I would've begged someone to pull the trigger and allow me to go with her. Just the thought of losing her filled me with such sorrow I could hardly put one foot in front of the other.

"Beau. Let go," she whispered and looked down at the fingers I had a near death grip on.

"I'm sorry, my love." I loosened my hold, but I *would not* let go. I'd *never* let go.

"Hey, I've got news for you, Sam," said Decker, who then pointed at Cord. "And you're lucky to be alive, you idiot. You don't fire a gun when there are nine other guys standing there, ready to shoot somebody."

Cord hung his head and didn't say anything. Attempting to defend his actions would've only made Decker angrier.

"You don't deserve this, Wheaton, but Sam, you're officially related to this putz."

She turned to me, literally beaming with happiness. It was hard to imagine that, a short while ago, a madman had nearly killed her.

"That means I'm related to Cena, right?" she asked, looking from me to Decker.

"Good chance of it," he responded. "I have a feeling you'll get confirmation of that very soon."

An alert went off on my mobile along with many others in the vicinity. I couldn't care less what it might be. I could not think about anything besides getting Sam inside, taking her up to the bedroom, and making love to her for several days straight.

"Juni's here," said Deck. "And Creola is right behind her."

"Were we expecting him?" Sam asked me.

"To be honest, my mind is entirely muddled. However, I don't believe so."

"What in the world is going on?" Juni asked, running over to us. "There were cop cars and an ambulance racing down Route 20. Grayson called and said somebody told him something went on here."

"It's a bit of a long story, if you don't mind—" I groaned when Mr. Creola exited his vehicle and hurried over to us.

"I heard on the police scanner. Suspect apprehended. Was it Jimmy Rooker?" he asked between taking several deep breaths.

"It was," Decker responded.

"If you'll excuse us, Samantha and I are going to—"

"Wait!" the attorney shouted. "I have something very important to tell you."

"Can't you tell us tomorrow?" I practically whined.

"Beau. Let him tell us." One look in Sam's imploring eyes, and I caved. I'd spend the rest of my life doing whatever she wanted, the very minute she wanted it.

"Let's go inside," she said.

"Should I, um, well, I'll come back another time," stammered Juni.

"Mr. Creola, is there any reason she has to leave?"

"None at all."

I refused to let go of Sam's hand as we climbed the steps, went in the front door, then as we walked over to the dining table.

"Beau, please," she whispered, shaking her hand free. I let it go but put my hand on her back as she sat in the chair I'd managed to pull out for her. As soon as I sat beside her, I reached for her hand again. When she looked at me and smiled, my heart melted.

"I love you so much," I whispered.

"I love you, Beau," she whispered back.

"As I said, I have important things to tell you."

The attorney glared at Decker when he took the seat beside him. I had a feeling he was only sitting in to annoy the poor man.

"The judge denied the request for injunction."

"Great," said Sam with little enthusiasm.

I squeezed her hand.

"And that means I can give you this." He passed an envelope to her. Inside was a key, Cena's death certificate, as well as a document certifying that Samantha was the sole beneficiary of Cena's trust. "I'm not sure what went on here today, but visiting the bank *can* wait until tomorrow. Although I'm going to suggest you go as soon as possible."

My eyes met Sam's. As much as I wanted to be alone with her, we'd have forever to do that. "Whatever you wish to do, my love."

"I'd like to go now."

I stood to pull out her chair but looked at the attorney. "Is there more?"

He shook his head. "I'll be available if you have questions."

"I have one, Paul," said Decker.

Mr. Creola sighed and turned in his direction.

"How long have you known Sam was Cena's great-granddaughter?"

Rather than answer Decker, the man turned to Samantha. "There *is* a letter from Mrs. Covert in the box. It explains everything."

Samantha and I rode in the backseat of the SUV. Cord drove, and Juni was in the passenger seat for moral support, as they said, should Sam need it. I was grateful to him for driving. Shock, adrenaline, fear, relief, and love coursed through my veins. If it weren't for my darling Sam's hands in mine, I had no doubt they would be shaking.

"Would you like me to come inside with you?" I asked when Cord pulled up to the bank.

"Has there been any part of this I've done without you?"

I thought for a moment. "I don't suppose there has been."

"Why would I start now?"

I actually felt like a bit of a wanker, given Sam appeared perfectly fine, unaffected, and she'd been the one in grave danger. As I got out of the SUV and came around to open her door, I told myself to buck up and be there for her, rather than fret over myself. Actually, I think it was my mum's voice I heard speaking in my head.

When we presented the documents to the bank manager and he asked Sam to follow him to the vault, I hesitated. She was two steps away, but came back, took my hand, and pulled me with her.

"Would you like me to do that?" I asked when Sam's hand shook trying to put in the second key that would allow the bank manager to open the box.

"Would you?"

"I'll leave you to view the contents. Just press that blue button when you're finished, and I'll come back." He had his hand on the door. "Just don't press the red button."

Once he left, I said, "What do you suppose it does? He didn't say, did he?"

Both Sam and I burst out laughing. "Little does he know that is the last thing someone should say to you." She rolled her eyes, then leaned forward and kissed me.

I couldn't speak for her, but a couple of minutes of laughter helped alleviate some of my stress.

"Are you certain you want me here while you do this?"

My darling Samantha glared at me. "Are you seriously going to make me say it *again*?"

"All right. My apologies," I said, holding up both my hands.

"Here goes."

I watched Sam remove an envelope, reach inside, and pull out a handwritten letter.

29

Sam

I gently unfolded the letter I knew would change my life. I'd never be Samantha Marquez, the girl who had no idea where she came from, again. Taking a deep breath, I began reading.

Dear Samantha,

I'm sure you have many questions, for which I have at least some answers.

To begin, I was ninety-seven years old when I found out I had a granddaughter and great-granddaughter. Tragically, I learned your mother, Madeline, had passed away only weeks before. But there was you, and you, I would protect.

While I could never prove it, I believe the accident that took my precious son's life was not one at all. I believe he was murdered. I also believed that if I made contact with you, if anyone learned of your existence before my death, you would also be in danger.

Know that if you are reading this, the threat to you is no longer.

I have a confession to make to you, and I will not try to explain why I did what I did or give excuses. It is my life's biggest regret, the one thing I would take back if only I could.

My dear son, Manley, who was named for his father, loved your grandmother very much. It was only after I spent years watching him relentlessly search for her that I realized the depth of that love. He never married, never had the family he didn't know existed. Never had happiness. All because of me.

I am the one who drove Pilar away. Forced her to leave. Thus, destroying five lives.

I believed she wasn't good enough for Manley, believed she only wanted his money. I learned differently when I discovered she hadn't taken what I offered her to leave. I thought to pay her off to prove to my son she didn't truly love him. In truth, she loved him far more than I did. She loved him enough to never tell him the horrible thing I did. She allowed him to live his life believing his mother was a good person. That this is the one and only time I confessed this sin is proof that I am not.

I have many regrets, but none bigger than not allowing my son to love who he wanted to, the way he wanted to, where he wanted to. If I had, I would've known the one thing I never did—the joy of grandchildren. Instead, I lived the rest of my life alone after my son's death. I had endless hours of utter loneliness to think about the mistakes I made.

I lost so much—my husband, my daughter, and my son—and you and your mother too. I can assure you, all the money in the world could never make up for any of those losses.

I died a very wealthy but very unhappy woman. I tell you this, not so you will feel sorry for me, but to assure you that I have paid heavily for my sins.

I know much about you, Samantha, but I don't know you at all. Another regret. It does not change what I wish for you, though.

If I had the power to give you anything besides the material things you now possess, it would be love. I pray your heart is open to it, and if not yet, that it will be soon.

Follow your heart, and do not let anyone stand in your way of doing so. And while my fervent dream is that you will love the Lilacs as much as I have since the day my husband brought me to it, it should not be an encumbrance.

My attorney will help with any decision you make. Whether you want to make it your home and fill it with the love and laughter it's never known or if you choose not to remain, you will not be judged.

I am a very old woman and fear I'm rambling now. There are journals I kept over the years beneath this letter. They are there for you to read if you want to know more about the family you never had the chance to meet.

I would ask for forgiveness, but I know I don't deserve it.
Your great-grandmother,
Cena Rooker Covert

I held the letter out to Beau, who took it.

"This is dated the twenty-fourth of December."

I nodded. "The day before she died."

He set the letter on the table, opened his arms to me, and held me while I cried.

Epilogue

Sam

Four months later

Beau and I spent countless hours reading Cena's journals and letters, and sorting through her photos. With his help and Juni's, I was able to piece together my family history.

There were letters Manley Jr. received from private detectives he'd hired, each one telling him they were sorry, but they could not find proof that Pilar Marquez had ever existed. The last letter, the one that said they'd finally found Pilar, her daughter, and granddaughter, arrived just days after he'd died.

After the snow melted, we visited the cemeteries where generations of both Coverts and Rookers were buried. I'd spent so much time looking at all the photos that, when I visited some of the graves, I could picture the person in my mind. It was odd, meeting your relatives after they were dead, but that was what it felt like I was doing.

Juni gave me a copy of Cena's favorite books, and sometimes, I'd go sit by her gravestone and read to her.

Beau always came with me, sat by my side, held my hand, and continued reading when I was too choked up with emotion to continue.

There were still mysteries left unsolved. Like why Ursula, my grandmother's sister, had left her husband when her twin boys, Jimmy and Johnny, were only three years old. I suppose it explained, in part, why she'd never told Manley how to find my grandmother.

The other thing no one could figure out was why Patricia Rooker, Cord's mother, had never told her children about the family she left behind in East Aurora or even why she'd left. I knew Cord was disappointed I hadn't found a single photo labeled with her name or any mention of her in Cena's journals.

We never met Hoss Schultz, but he sent a letter, terminating the contract between Schultz Wineries and Lilac Lane. It was dated the day after Jimmy Rooker was taken away in an ambulance before being charged with attempted murder.

From that day on, Beau and I ran the winery, as we'd planned to anyway. He'd increased the hectares devoted to grape growing in time for spring plant-ing, and we hoped to double our production within five years.

"There are my beloveds."

I looked up at the smiling face of the man who tomorrow would become my husband. He kissed my forehead and scratched Wanda's ears.

"I'm so glad we decided to get married here in East Aurora. It feels right, you know?"

Beau smiled. "It's home—our home."

"It is, isn't it?"

"On the subject of our wedding, I've a gift for you."

"Beau, you didn't have to get me a gift. I'm ashamed to admit I didn't get anything for you."

He shook his head. "How wrong you are, my beloved Samantha. You've given me far more than you'll ever know."

I smiled through my tears. "Without you, I wouldn't have come here. I would've lived the rest of my life believing I was alone in the world—" I shook my head when emotion made it too hard to speak. "You've given me everything," I managed to whisper. "Everything."

Beau brushed away my tears. "To be honest, this gift is something I picked up some time ago." My eyes scrunched when he put the key fob for the SUV in my hand. "Since we've decided to live in New York State full time, you'll need to register it here." He pulled a piece of paper from his pocket and handed it to me.

"This is the title."

"That, it is."

"It has my name on it."

Beau nodded, leaned forward, and kissed me. "Given we'll be joined in marriage tomorrow and are residing in a community property state, you cannot get angry with me about this. What's mine is yours, and vice versa."

I shook my head.

"No?" his forehead scrunched.

I waved my hand. "All of this—the house, the Lilacs, the winery, everything—I'll gladly share with you. But the SUV? Sorry, Beau, it's mine."

He smiled. "I see. Which means, then, the Porsche is mine."

I tapped my lip. "Hmm. In that case…"

He wriggled his eyebrows. "I let you drive mine if you let me drive yours?"

"First, we have to get yours here, and I have to clean out my apartment, which means—"

Beau stopped me with a kiss. "Already taken care of."

"How?"

"The better question would be who."

"Alex?"

He smiled. "None other."

Most of our friends from California had already arrived for the wedding. Beau's father would be here this afternoon, as would his brother, Press, and his wife. The wedding ceremony was being held at St. John's Lutheran Church, and the reception would take place here, at the Lilacs—where plants bearing flowers by the same name lined the driveway and surrounded the house and the winery.

Sadly, Cru and Daphne each sent their regrets, separately. I'd asked Beau if he talked to either one, and he said he hadn't and changed the subject.

"You'll have to get a new one of those soon," Beau said, motioning to the journal I'd started keeping the day after I sat in the bank vault and first read Cena's letter.

"I'm very happy we made the decision to stay here," said Beau, looking out the window at the view of the grounds.

"Me too."

He rested both hands on my abdomen, then leaned forward and kissed it. "And hello to you too, my baby beloved," he whispered.

No one besides Beau and I knew, but in just a few months, we'd add to the love and laughter Cena hoped would fill the house.

Keep reading for a sneak peek

at the first book in Heather Slade's

Roaring Fork Ranch series,

Roaring Fork Wrangler

He came to save his family's legacy.
She stayed by his side.
Together, they'll uncover secrets
that could tear them apart.

CORD

I thought spending a year in East Aurora would be the worst thing that could happen to me. Then I met Juniper Chance, and suddenly, leaving seemed impossible. But when someone tries to kill me, I realize there's more to my family's past than I ever knew. As I fight to heal and uncover the truth, I risk losing the one person who's become my reason for staying. Can I solve the mystery of my mother's past and keep Juni by my side, or will the secrets of the Lilacs estate tear us apart forever?

JUNI

I never expected to fall for a cowboy from Colorado, especially one who's only here temporarily. But Cord Wheaton stole my heart from the moment we met.

When he nearly dies, I'm forced to confront my own painful past as I help him recover. Now, as we unravel the mysteries surrounding his attack and his mother's history in East Aurora, I'm torn between protecting my heart and fighting for our future. Will the truth bring us closer together, or drive Cord away for good?

1

Cord

"Juni's here," I heard someone say when my phone beeped, signaling an arrival requesting access to the estate.

I looked down at the screen and caught a glimpse of her before she rolled up her window and drove through the gate. Just the briefest of glances of Juniper Chance had my pulse racing and the crotch of my jeans tightening.

I'd had the same reaction the first time I met her and every time I was in her presence since.

Yeah, it had been a while since I was with a woman, but none I'd met since arriving in this small Western New York village had the same effect on me. Plenty had been damned attractive, too.

"What in the world is going on?" Juni asked, jumping out of her car and running over to us. I heard her say her brother had called with news that something was going down at the Lilacs estate.

While I could hear her words, they weren't registering with the same intensity as her plump red lips. Damn if I didn't want to wrap my arm around her waist, pull her body close to mine, and kiss the living shit out of her.

"Are you okay?" she asked.

When I realized she was speaking directly to me, I looked into her eyes. "Yeah, why?"

"Just…um…nothing." Her cheeks flushed.

I followed her gaze and turned to watch everyone but the two of us go inside.

"Should we join them?" she asked.

"Not too sure I'm welcome," I said, stuffing my hands in my pockets.

Her eyes widened. "Why not?"

I kicked at the dirt. "I shot Jimmy Rooker."

While I had no idea what I expected her reaction to be, it wasn't the board smile that cracked her face. "He was such an asshole. Way beyond that, actually."

"Still is, darlin'. I shot his kneecap out."

"I guess it makes me a terrible person that I was happy thinking he was dead."

"No doubt plenty of people would agree with you." I motioned toward the porch steps. "You wanna go inside?"

Juni nodded, and I walked in that direction.

"Wait," I heard her say.

When I turned around, she was right behind me.

"What were you thinking about before? You know, when I asked if you were okay."

I sighed and looked up at the canopy of trees above us. If I said I couldn't remember, I'd be lying. "Might not be somethin' you're interested in knowin'."

"You're wrong. I mean, I am interested in whatever it was."

My eyes bored into hers, and I took a step closer. "You're sure?"

She moistened her lips with her tongue.

I raised my fingers to her chin. "Don't do that, darlin'."

"Why not?"

"Because lickin' your lips was what I was thinking about."

Keep reading for a sneak peek at the next

book in Heather Slade's

Wicked Winemakers

Central Coast Second Label series,

Cru's Crush

**He's waited in the wings while she loved another.
She's finally realized who she really wanted.
Together, they'll harvest a love
that's been growing all along.**

CRU

I've loved Daphne Cullen for as long as I can remember. When she finally joined our family winery, it felt like all my dreams were coming true. But just as we found happiness together, fate tore us apart. Now she's halfway around the world, fighting to save her family's business. I'm desperate to be with her, but I have responsibilities here. Can our love survive the distance, or will it wither on the vine?

DAPHNE

Working alongside Cru Avila at his family's winery was everything I'd ever wanted. Our passion for winemaking and each other seemed perfect—until my father's stroke called me back to Australia. Now I'm torn between my family's needs and the man I love. Cru is my soulmate, but our lives are on opposite sides of the world. Is our love strong enough to bridge the distance, or will we have to let each other go?

1

Cru

I stood in the shadows, watching Daphne pick up a frame and study the photo inside. I couldn't see it from where I stood, but I still knew whose image she studied—Beau Barrett, the man who was both my best friend and my nemesis, but only where the woman in front of me was concerned.

Beau and Daphne had been one of those on-again, off-again couples since they were teenagers. Every time they broke up, I hoped it would be long enough for me to have a chance with her.

I nearly toppled over when someone nudged my shoulder, and I glanced behind me at my older brother Brix.

He shook his head. "You gotta give it up, man," he whispered. "Beau will be back before you know it."

I led him down the hallway and into a bedroom, then shut the door behind us. "Not this time, bro."

Brix rested against the wall and smirked. "You keep tellin' yourself that. How long have you been crushin' on Daphne Cullen? Ten years? More?"

"Things are different now. Beau is with Samantha Marquez." Frankly, I was surprised he didn't know, given his wife, Addy, and Sam were best friends.

Brix chuckled. "Not a chance. There's no way Sam would put up with his shit." His expression changed. "Wait. Do you know where Beau is?"

Shortly after his mother's funeral, Beau had disappeared, and until I saw him in New York, I'd had no idea where he was, either. Turned out he was with Sam.

"I'm telling you; it's serious between them."

Brix pushed himself from the wall. "So where is he?"

"C'mon, don't ask me that. He's with Sam. That's all I can tell you right now."

"What makes you think they're serious?" Brix shook his head. "No offense at all to Sam, but I just don't see her with Beau."

I held up my phone so he could see the text I'd just received from our brother Salazar, who everyone called Snapper.

"No shit! Beau proposed and Sam said yes?" Brix practically shouted at the same time someone pushed the door open. When he moved out of the way, I came face-to-face with Daphne.

She spun around and raced off in the opposite direction, but not before I saw tears fill her eyes.

Brix grabbed my arm when I walked past him. "Let her go."

I shook my head and pulled away from his grasp. "I can't."

My brother stood in front of the door, blocking my exit. He put his hands on my shoulders. "This is going to sound corny as hell, but, Cru, you're supposed to be the leading lady, not the best friend, and for some reason, you're acting like, you know, the best friend."

I took a step back from my brother. "What the fuck are you talking about, Brix? The leading lady?"

"It's from a movie Addison and I watched last night. You get my point, though. You need to stop acting like the best friend so Daphne can see you as the leading lady—err, man."

I shook my head and walked over to the window. As I could've predicted, Daphne was walking on the beach, alone. Even from here, I knew she was crying.

Brix approached and stood next to me. "If you go out there now, she'll cry on your shoulder, Cru. You'll console her, and it'll be just another conversation about her and Beau. The next time you talk to her, it needs to change. No more her and Beau. Make it about her and you."

"Like it's that easy."

"Take it from me; it is if you want it bad enough." He turned to look at me. "Do you?"

"I've loved her for as long as Beau has," I murmured.

"Wrong. You've loved her when Beau never did. Now, convince her of that."

I faced my brother and stared into his eyes. "What should I do?"

"Leave."

About the Author

USA Today best-selling author Heather Slade writes shamelessly sexy, edge-of-your seat romantic suspense.

She gave herself the gift of writing a book for her own birthday one year. Sixty-plus books later (and counting), she's having the time of her life.

The women Slade writes are self-confident, strong, with wills of their own, and hearts as big as the Colorado sky. The men are sublimely sexy, seductive alphas who rise to the challenge of capturing the sweet soul of a woman whose heart they'll hold in the palm of their hand forever. Add in a couple of neck-snapping twists and turns, a page-turning mystery, and a swoon-worthy HEA, and you'll be holding one of her books in your hands.

She loves to hear from her readers. You can contact her at heather@heatherslade.com

To keep up with her latest news and releases, please visit her website at www.heatherslade.com to sign up for her newsletter.

MORE FROM AUTHOR HEATHER SLADE

ROMANTIC SUSPENSE

K19 SECURITY
SOLUTIONS
TEAM ONE
Razor's Edge
Gunner's Redemption
Mistletoe's Magic
Mantis' Desire
Dutch's Salvation

K19 SECURITY
SOLUTIONS
TEAM TWO
Striker's Choice
Monk's Fire
Halo's Oath
Tackle's Honor
Onyx's Awakening

K19 SHADOW
OPERATIONS
TEAM ONE
Code Name: Ranger
Code Name: Diesel
Code Name: Wasp
Code Name: Cowboy
Code Name: Mayhem

K19 ALLIED
INTELLIGENCE
TEAM ONE
Code Name: Ares
Code Name: Cayman
Code Name: Poseidon
Code Name: Zeppelin
Code Name: Magnet

K19 ALLIED
INTELLIGENCE
TEAM TWO
Code Name: Puck
*Code Name:
Michelangelo*
Code Name: Typhon
Code Name: Hornet
Code Name: Reaper

K19 GENESIS
CONSORTIUM
TEAM ONE
Blackjack's Ascent
Dagger's Shield
Sundance's Trail
Nomad's Compass
Preacher's Decree

K19 SENTINEL
CYBER
TEAM ONE
Code Name: Admiral
Code Name: Dante
Code Name: Grit
Code Name: Tank
Code Name: Atticus

K19 SENTINEL
CYBER
TEAM TWO
Code Name: Kodiak
Code Name: Paragon
Code Name: Vex
Code Name: Shredder
Code Name: Jagger

PROTECTORS
UNDERCOVER
TEAM ONE
Undercover Agent
Undercover Emissary
Undercover Savior
Undercover Infidel
Undercover Shadow

ROYAL AGENTS
OF MI6
Make Me Shiver
Drive Me Wilder
Feel My Pinch
Chase My Shadow
Find My Angel

THE INVINCIBLES
TEAM ONE
Code Name: Deck
Code Name: Edge
Code Name: Grinder
Code Name: Rile
Code Name: Smoke

THE INVINCIBLES
TEAM TWO
Code Name: Buck
Code Name: Irish
Code Name: Saint
Code Name: Hammer
Code Name: Rip

THE
UNSTOPPABLES
TEAM ONE
Code Name: Fury
Code Name: Merried

MORE FROM AUTHOR HEATHER SLADE

WINE COUNTRY ROMANCE

BUTLER RANCH
Kade's Worth
Brodie's Promise
Maddox's Truce
Naughton's Secret
Mercer's Vow
Kade's Return
Butler Ranch Christmas

WICKED WINEMAKERS
CENTRAL COAST
FIRST LABEL
Brix's Bid
Ridge's Release
Press' Passion
Zin's Sins
Tryst's Temptation

WICKED WINEMAKERS
CENTRAL COAST
SECOND LABEL
Beau's Beloved
Cru's Crush
Bit's Bliss
Snapper's Seduction
Kick's Kiss

WICKED WINEMAKERS
RUSSIAN RIVER VALLEY
FIRST LABEL
Bas' Blend
Hux's Harvest
Wolf's Want
Oak's Vintage
Cooper's Claim

COWBOY ROMANCE

COWBOYS OF
CRESTED BUTTE
A Cowboy Falls
A Cowboy's Dance
A Cowboy's Kiss
A Cowboy Stays
A Cowboy Wins

ROARING FORK RANCH
Roaring Fork Wrangler
Roaring Fork Roughstock
Roaring Fork Rockstar
Roaring Fork Rooker
Roaring Fork Bridger

SANGRE VISTA RANCH
Thorn's Stand
Stetson's Storm
Maverick's Reckoning
Cinch's Wager
Flints Chance

HEATHER SLADE WRITING AS
MERRIGAN CALDER

DARK ROMANCE
THORNED THISTLE
Commanded

Possessed

Obsessed

Captured

Surrendered

NEW SERIES COMING SOON
CRIMSON CHALICE
VELVET VIPER